# Harry the Hypno-potamus
## Metaphorical Tales for the Treatment of Children

Linda Thomson PhD MSN CPNP

Crown House Publishing Limited
www.crownhouse.co.uk

First published by

Crown House Publishing Ltd
Crown Buildings, Bancyfelin, Carmarthen, Wales, SA33 5ND, UK
www.crownhouse.co.uk

and

Crown House Publishing Company LLC
4 Berkeley Street, 1st Floor, Norwalk, CT 06850, USA
www.CHPUS.com

Illustrations © Kidz Book Design

**British Library of Cataloguing-in-Publication Data**

A catalogue entry for this book is available from the British Library.

**International Standard Book Number 1904424570**

**Library of Congress Control Number 2004111436**

Printed and bound in the UK by *Cambridge Printing*

To my husband, George O. Thomson for his lasting and unwavering love, encouragement, and belief in me. He is my soul-mate, best friend, and ardent supporter.

To my life's greatest blessings, my children: Marshall, Brenton, Amanda and her husband, Wade; and Haley, my precious first grandchild, and, hopefully, not my last.

To my mentor, Dr. Dan Kohen, my own master teacher, who has shared his gifts of wisdom and spirit with me and with so many others. Through Dan's encouragement, he instills confidence that all things are possible, including a book.

# Contents

# The Tales for Children

# Acknowledgements

I stand on the shoulders of all those who came before me in the field of hypnosis, and generously shared their wisdom and expertise with me. I am grateful for these guiding lights. I hope through my tales that I can help others to help children help themselves by using hypnosis.

All of the animal and human characters in the book are named for people who inspired and taught me how to use hypnosis more effectively in my work with children. They are luminaries in the field of hypnosis. I thank them for their wisdom and inspiration.

Milton Erickson MD (Milton) brought hypnosis back into the therapeutic realm. He founded the American Society for Clinical Hypnosis.

David Gottsegen MD (Davey) is the pediatrician who introduced me to the field of pediatric hypnotherapy.

Dan Kohen MD (Dr. Dan), a developmental and behavioral pediatrician, has been an incredible teacher, mentor, and friend.

Karen Olness MD (Ol'Ness) and Dan Kohen wrote *the* book on pediatric hypnosis: *Hypnosis and Hypnotherapy with Children*. Karen's seminal work in pediatric hypnosis has been an inspiration.

Candy Erickson MD (Candy) is a pediatrician who teaches hypnosis workshops for the Society for Developmental and Behavioral Pediatrics. She encouraged me to illustrate one of my metaphors and turn it into my first children's book, *The Magic Carpet*.

Claire Frederick MD (Claire), a former editor of the *American Journal of Clinical Hypnosis*, believed that I could write and had something to say.

Rebecca Kajander MSN CPNP (Becky) is a friend and kindred spirit. Becky was perhaps the first nurse practitioner to incorporate both biofeedback and hypnosis to help children help themselves.

D. Corydon Hammond PhD (Cory) is the editor of "the big red book", *Handbook of Hypnotic Suggestions and Metaphors*. It is the bible for clinicians who incorporate hypnotherapy into their practice.

Larry Sugarman MD (Sugar Man) is the pediatrician who created "Imaginative Medicine", a video that demonstrates how hypnosis can be incorporated into everyday clinical practice.

Norma Barretta, PhD and Phil Barretta, MS (Norma and Phil) are gifted clinicians and educators who have taught us much about the language of hypnosis.

Mitch Smith MSW (Mitch) and Richard Garver EdD (Garver) have generously shared with me their knowledge of sports psychology and mental skills training for athletes.

Jordan Zarren MSW (Jordan) taught me about magic, hypnosis and kids.

Donald Brown MD (Brownie) and Marlene Hunter MD (Marlene) are Canadian physicians who incorporate hypnosis into their practices and generously share their wisdom with others. Marlene taught me about creating a WIB, that in this book became a WIFT.

David Wark PhD (Wark) developed "alert hypnosis", and taught me how to use the technique.

Jeff Lazarus MD (Lazarus) is a pediatrician with a great sense of humor who always makes me smile.

Adrienne Peltz-London LCSWR (Adrienne) is a social worker who uses hypnosis to help her clients live their lives despite their cancer and die with dignity.

Olafur Palsson PsyD (Olafur) is a leading clinician and researcher who investigates the use of hypnosis in treating patients with irritable bowel syndrome.

Thom Lobe MD (Dr. Thom) is a pediatric surgeon who helps children feel better so they can heal faster after surgery.

David Spiegel MD and his father, Herbert Spiegel MD (Spiegel) are eminent researchers in the field of hypnosis.

Kay Thompson DDS (Dr. Kay), a dentist, championed the use of hypnosis in dentistry.

Robert Deutsch PhD (Dr. Deutsch), Julie Linden PhD (Julie), and Valerie Wall PhD (Valerie) are all gifted child psychologists.

Pat Burbridge RN MSN (Pat); Mary Herring RN MSN (Mary); Pam Kaiser PhD CPNP, (Pam); Kathryn Landon-Malone MSN CPNP (Kathryn); Zendi Moldenhauer PhD CPNP (Zendi); and Allen Moulton RN MS (Allen) are all nursing colleagues who pioneered in incorporating hypnosis into nursing practice.

Elgan Baker PhD (Elgan); Sheryll Daniel PhD (Sheryll); Molly Delaney PsyD (Molly); Gary Elkins PhD (Elkins); Dabney Ewin MD (Dabney);  Daniel Handel MD (Handel); Donald Lynch MD (Lynch); Charles Mutter MD (Mutter); Marc Oster PsyD (Oster); Max Shapiro PhD (Max); Jody Thomas PhD ( Jody); Rick Voit PhD (Voit); Tom Wall PhD (Tom); and Lonnie Zeltzer MD (Lonnie) have all shared with me and with many others the wisdom of their experience in helping patients to help themselves with hypnosis.

# Foreword

### by Karen Olness and Daniel Kohen

*Harry the Hypno-potamus* is a remarkable book. Written by a creative and committed pediatric nurse practitioner, it is for both adults and children and is both serious and whimsical. It is informative and hopeful. Any child-health professional who appreciates hypnosis will enjoy reading *Harry the Hypno-potamus*. We believe that children will be encouraged and given confidence that they themselves can contribute to a solution of their own problems.

This book includes a detailed introduction for pediatric health and mental health professionals. This provides a detailed description of metaphors, and describes common problems of children for which the metaphorical tales of animals may be helpful. The introduction explains thoughtfully how the metaphorical tales may be used therapeutically while also allowing for and encouraging the clinician/reader to use their own creativity in adapting and applying the stories and metaphors with individual children. For example, the tales of the koala, gazelle, warthog, and turtle concern anxiety. The jaguar, walrus, elephant, otter, and gorilla all have fears. The story of Claire Koala is used to teach diaphragmatic breathing as an induction technique. The story of Molly Macaw described a metaphor for trichotillomania, i.e. Molly pulled out her tail feathers. And Harry the Hypno-potamus helped her to use her imagination to solve the problem of feather pulling. The problems of the animal characters include performance anxiety, thumb sucking, nail biting, tics, enuresis, encopresis, bruxism, chronic pain, OCD, irritable bowel syndrome, asthma, diabetes, epilepsy, and leukemia. There is a coatimundi (an animal who is native to Belize) with a fatal illness.

The coatimundi learns to use his imagination to go on wonderful trips and to prepare for death as the greatest trip.

This book also includes a handout section that can be given to parents. It provides important clarifying information about hypnosis, and explains that hypnosis should only be used as part of a treatment plan for a specific problem after a careful evaluation by a trained health professional.

The purpose of the metaphorical stories is to introduce children to hypnosis and the power of their imagination. We believe that the average child will be easily engaged by these interesting stories and will learn from them. Some children will want to read the stories for themselves, and others will want them read by others. The author has fashioned the stories to be not only powerful therapeutically, but to have the built in flexibility to be utilized by children, parents, and clinicians in a variety of ways. The author has used these metaphorical stories in her practice for several years and her recommendations to colleagues are based on many successful experiences with them.

Child-health professionals who use hypnosis have received a wonderful gift from Linda Thomson. The book is fun; most of the animals are named after health care professionals who use hypnotherapy with their young patients. Her creativity is a treasure for us and allows us to expand our various therapeutic armamentaria. The basis for her stories is solid. How rare it is to read a serious book about hypnosis and to laugh aloud in the process!

# Preface

### *Imagination is a gift you give yourself*

In my teens, I was critically injured in a catastrophic skiing accident. As a result, I spent three months in an intensive care unit, on life support and hemodialysis, fighting for my life and breath. Hypnosis could have been extraordinarily helpful during that ordeal, if only someone could have shown me the techniques to use.

I have been a pediatric nurse practitioner for thirty years. The children I have most enjoyed working with in my practice were the ones most other providers didn't want: those who came in kicking and screaming, the ones who hid under the examination table, afraid to come out; the teenager who had been sexually abused and needed a pelvic examination; the child in pain, in respiratory distress, or with a terminal illness. Partly due to my own experience, I seemed to have a knack for working with these children. After attending a lecture on hypnosis and hypnotherapy in pediatrics, I realized that many of the techniques I successfully used with children were hypnotic ones, and I wanted to learn how to build on my experience.

I received my training in hypnosis through the Society for Developmental and Behavioral Pediatrics, the American Society of Clinical Hypnosis, the Society for Clinical and Experimental Hypnosis, and the International Society of Hypnosis. I am now an Approved Consultant in Clinical Hypnosis.

Hypnosis, I discovered, is still a misunderstood and underutilized resource for health and healing. I decided to do my part to change that. The topic of my doctoral dissertation, published in the American Journal of Clinical Hypnosis, was "A Project to Change the Attitudes, Beliefs and Practices of Health Care Professionals Concerning Hypnosis." My research demonstrated that teaching colleagues about hypnosis can make a difference in their behavior and how they think about hypnotic intervention therapy.

I wrote the story of "How Harry the Hypno-potamus Got His Name" to introduce children to hypnosis and the power of their imagination. Harry was subsequently joined by a multitude of zoo friends who all had their own physical and psychological problems. These metaphorical tales incorporate many of the techniques that I have found to be helpful in my work with children. Through reading this book, I hope that others can learn the language of hypnotic techniques, metaphorical strategies, and healing so they can empower children to help themselves.

The book is divided into two sections—a "Clinical Section" designed to explain the use of the stories, and "The Tales for Children"—the actual stories themselves that can be read to the children or can be personalized and adapted to the clinician's individual style.

# Clinical Section

# *Introduction*

This book is written for pediatric health and mental health professionals who have an understanding of child development and previous training in hypnotherapy. *Harry the Hypno-potamus* contains metaphors that deal with a variety of physical and behavioral problems. Imbedded in each metaphor are hypnotherapeutic techniques that can be used as part of a comprehensive approach to the diagnosis and treatment of certain disorders.

Reading the first story, "How Harry the Hypno-potamus Got His Name", to a child is a wonderful introduction to hypnosis and the power of imagination. The stories in the rest of the book are about different animals that all live in the Ashland Zoo. Each has a physical or emotional problem and learns specific hypnotherapeutic techniques and self-regulatory strategies to help master it.

The clinician may choose to either read one of the stories with a child, or adapt the techniques to his own unique style. Some of the therapeutic interventions are very problem-specific; others are more general and can be used for a variety of conditions. The developmental age of the child must also be taken into account, as well as his or her cognitive and perceptual skills, so the clinician can adapt the induction, language, and hypnotic techniques to the child's developmental level.

Contained within some of the stories are hypnotic scripts. Pacing, leading, cadence, rhythm, and vocal inflections are all important in hypnosis. In the scripted portion of the tales, the words that deserve emphasis in a hypnotic intervention are in bold face type.

## Pediatric Hypnosis

An integral part of play is imagining and pretending. For most children, an altered state of consciousness is familiar, comfortable, and easy to achieve. Children need to explore and experience their surroundings. They want to engage with others and their environment. They are relentlessly curious about the how and why of objects, people, situations and themselves, and have an urge for mastery and control. Endless possibilities are open to them through their inner world of imagination. A child can employ fantasy to change or avoid an unpleasant situation, gratify unmet needs, remember the past, or invent the future.

Children want to be happy, healthy, comfortable and successful. When physical, mental or environmental conditions interfere, a child may develop maladaptive behavior, either consciously or unconsciously. During a therapeutic alliance, hypnotherapy can be a very powerful tool for a clinician who is invested in helping the child experience success, comfort and health. The hypnotherapeutic work enhances and strengthens the child's natural strivings toward exploration, social relationships, fantasy, and creativity.

Children want to experience life to the greatest extent possible; therefore, cultivating a child's imagination with hypnosis is not only appealing, but effective. The success of a hypnotherapeutic approach to treatment depends on several factors that can be remembered by the acronymn **AH CREAM** (see next page). The most important one is rapport. The strength of the therapeutic alliance between child and clinician is critical. The child needs to feel safe and able to trust the professional. An accurate assessment of the problem, including a thorough history, is necessary. The clinician must be not only competent, and confident that he or she can help the child, but credentialed as well. A health professional should not use hypnosis to treat a condition that she is not qualified to treat without hypnosis. The child needs to expect that the hypnotherapy will be successful and actively participate in the process. Hypnosis is not something that is done to a child; it is something that the child does to and for himself, or allows to happen when he has set the goal he wishes to achieve. The child's motivation to change is another important variable in the success of the hypnotherapeutic intervention.

---

**AH CREAM**

**A:** Accurate assessment

**H:** History

**C:** Confidence, competence, and credentials

**R:** Rapport

**E:** Expectation

**A:** Active participation

**M:** Motivation

---

## Metaphorical Approaches

If a picture is worth a thousand words, then a metaphor is worth a million. Like parables, myths, and fairy tales, metaphors convey an idea in an indirect way by using symbolic language. Hypnosis is a right brain phenomenon, and the right brain is symbolic. Metaphor may well be the language of the right brain.

Throughout civilization, metaphors have been used as a teaching method. The parables of the Bible, the fairy tales of the Grimm brothers, and the fables of Aesop are all familiar to western cultures. As children, we learned the lessons of "The Little Engine That Could" and "The Hare and the Tortoise". Those tales had far greater impact than the verbal admonitions "don't give up" and "slow and steady wins the race" ever could.

Metaphors allow the hypnotherapist to communicate simultaneously with both the conscious and unconscious minds. The conscious mind processes the words, the story, and the ideas, while the therapeutic message is slipped into the unconscious via implication and connotation. The unconscious mind explores the broader meaning and the personalized relevance of the metaphor. In hypnosis, the wider meaning of the metaphor is never fully explained, so that the unconscious mind is left to explore just beyond the grasp of reason. It is this pursuit of personalized relevance that gives the metaphor its potency. When a hypnotherapist uses metaphors, the moral of the story is never explained, as it is in Aesop's fables, leaving the individual to figure out the meaning for herself—a much more powerful experience.

The potency of a metaphor is created through a right brain experience linking emotion, symbolic language, and life experience. The goal of the metaphor is to expand human consciousness. After Vogel and Bogen created a split brain by surgically transecting the *corpus collosum*\*, researchers learned a great deal about how the two hemispheres of the brain process information. Although the hemispheres process information cooperatively, each has its own unique style or specialization. The left brain works logically and literally to process the sequential coding of the printed word, while the right brain simultaneously processes language in a holistic, implicative, and imagistic fashion. Right-brain function is necessary to generate the imagery and glean the meaning of a story.

Metaphor appears to be the language of the right brain. When communication is metaphorical, the right hemisphere is activated, since this is the hemisphere that is more involved in processing subjective and sensory experiences. Psychosomatic symptoms are processed by predominately right brain functions; psychosomatic illness may be an expression in the language of the right brain. Since the comprehension of metaphors is a right brain phenomenon, using metaphors in hypnosis may be a means of communicating directly with the right brain in its own language. Metaphorical approaches to therapy may be much less time-intensive because of the right hemispheric mediation of both symptomatology and metaphorical meaning. Metaphors allow the hypnotherapist to speak symbolically to the unconscious mind.

Using metaphors in hypnosis effects change in a positive direction. Therapeutic suggestions may not be overtly obvious to the listener. The suggestion may be so cleverly entwined and embedded in the story that the child is unconsciously influenced to change without being consciously admonished to do so. This may result in a sense of accomplishment and a greater feeling of self-confidence. Through metaphors, the child may be exposed to new possibilities, new perspectives, and differing philosophies. Metaphors help to bypass resistance because they are subjectively experienced. The child views the problem as something that is happening to somebody else; therefore, she does not feel personally threatened.

Adding positive input to the unconscious is only one aim of metaphors. Metaphors replenish the soul. Because they are non-threatening, they often engage and enhance empowerment, causing children to stretch their minds, broaden their horizons, and develop wisdom. Metaphors help to change patterns of behavior by altering the individual's usual way of thinking.

Restating the child's problem in a non-threatening metaphor provides the patient with a different view of the situation. Reframing helps the child to take charge of mastering or resolving the problem. In reframing, the facts of a situation or an event remain the same, but the way the situation is viewed or conceptualized is changed, thereby altering the entire meaning. Sometimes it is necessary for the child to use senses or perceptions different from the ones he would ordinarily use to experience success. With metaphorical approaches, the child's unconscious mind is encouraged to develop novel ways to overcome limitations.

## Anxiety

Anxiety is a normal and universal human experience that results from a real or perceived danger, or a threat to safety. The individual may feel a loss of self-control, self-esteem, or self-efficacy. Physical symptoms that may result from anxiety include tachycardia, shortness of breath, dizziness, insomnia, avoidance behavior, tremulousness, and difficulty concentrating. In response to stress,

---

\*In the 1960s, neurosurgeons performed an experimental and unprecedented surgical procedure on a patient with epilepsy. They intentionally severed the nerve pathways between the two hemisperes of the brain. As a result scientists discovered that the right and left brain have their own unique style of processing information (Sperry, 1968).

children may experience headache, recurrent abdominal pain, nausea, and/or sleep disturbances.

In youngsters, anxiety is the most commonly occurring mental disorder, and one of the most easily treated with hypnosis. No one likes to feel anxious. Children are very receptive to learning new ways to regain a sense of control; they want to feel empowered to take charge of their bodies and their lives. Teaching children relaxation, mental imagery, and biofeedback is an effective therapeutic strategy. In addition, children may need psychopharmacologic therapy, counseling, psychodynamic psychotherapy, or cognitive behavioral therapy.

Anxiety may have a specific cause or be more generalized, without an objective focus. As a specific anxiety increases, the patient develops a fear. If the fear enlarges and begins to envelop day-to-day functioning, it becomes a phobia. Anxiety can instantaneously overwhelm some children's coping skills and result in panic. This triggers the release of adrenalin, resulting in unpleasant physical symptoms. The process may create a feedback loop that perpetuates the panic.

Anxiety is a problem of degree. It can be a desirable and appropriate response to a realistic danger; however, when the child's response is out of proportion to the actual threat, the anxiety can significantly disrupt his life. The longer the child's anxiety and fears remain untreated in the hope that he may outgrow them, the more difficult it may become to eradicate them. The relaxation response, frequently an integral part of hypnosis, can be extraordinarily beneficial, especially when combined with desensitization and ego strengthening. Visualizing success during hypnosis is a powerful technique to increase feelings of self-efficacy and control.

# Habit Disorders

A habit is a constant, often unconscious, inclination to repeatedly perform an action. The behavior may begin for a variety of reasons and initially serve an important purpose or function. A habit may result from stress or trauma. As the behavior is increasingly repeated, it becomes habituated, and may have nothing whatever to do with the initial trigger.

Some habit disorders may have adverse health effects. The child who has one may suffer humiliation and social rejection, resulting in low self-esteem. She may refuse to go to school. Medications with unpleasant side effects may be prescribed.

Many children have no desire to alter their repetitive behavior patterns. The behavior may provide comfort or a release from stress. "Ownership" of the habit can make the child feel powerful, or he may enjoy the way it aggravates his parent. Some children want desperately to stop their habit, but haven't any idea where to begin. They may have tried unsuccessfully to quit, and fear another failure.

Depending on the habit, hypnosis may be used as the primary treatment modality, or as an adjunctive therapy. Creating mindfulness about the habitual behavior is the first important step. A behavior is a habit only if it is something the child does without thinking about it. The hypnotic trance state decreases a patient's anxiety, and may be used to increase motivation and sense of control. Ego strengthening is part of every hypnotic strategy. It reinforces the child's confidence, sense of personal responsibility, and mastery.

Hypnosis has been used very successfully to control a variety of habit disorders in children. When a child is taught self-hypnosis, he has received an incredible gift. It is empowering for a child to control a habit that once controlled him. The child now owns the techniques and can use them whenever challenges arise throughout his lifetime.

## Pain

Hypnotic interventions for pain control began when the first mother kissed her child's booboo and made it all better. Pain is a complex phenomenon affected by temporal attributes of time and place, emotional connotations, and individual interpretation. Because pain is subjective, its experience can be altered. Each component of pain can be modified by the rapport, language, responsiveness and heightened psychophysiologic control that comprise the hypnotic experience. Hypnosis can empower a child to take charge of her life and her pain. It can reduce fear and anxiety about the pain, and help reframe a positive mental attitude. However, the essential ingredient in the hypnotic management of pain is the patient's positive expectation.

At any one time, there are multiple substructures of consciousness competing for our attention. Painful experiences demand dominance, asserting a powerful influence on conscious attention. When fantasy can pre-empt pain in the hierarchy of substructures, hypnosis is successful. Attending to one event reduces the attention to another that is competing with it; thus, the pain is dissociated from awareness.

Several factors can affect the child's perception of pain. Her age, developmental stage, and previous experience with pain are important. Gender, culture, and individual differences in coping styles may affect how the child expresses pain. The clinician needs to assess the emotional significance of the pain, and the child's physical and emotional state. Experiencing and relinquishing pain is both a psychological and physiological phenomenon. Nowhere is the mind–body connection so intricately woven as in the perception and control of pain.

When a child experiences acute pain, he is already in a heightened state of awareness. He focuses on the pain or injury directly and intensely. The child is highly motivated to seek relief, and thus is responsive to suggestions for comfort. The hypnotherapist can establish rapport and provide a focus for the child's already intensified attention. The calm and confidence of the hypnotherapist can foster a positive expectation that will assuage fear and doubt.

Chronic and recurrent pain differs from acute pain in several respects. With chronic pain there is a sense of negative expectancy. The child learns to expect the return of the pain even when it is gone. The expectation may turn to fear and dread, magnifying anxiety and a sense of despair and intensifying the perception of pain.

When hypnosis is employed to relieve pain, the careful use of language is critical. By carefully choosing her words and reframing the symptom, the hypnotherapist can create a new paradigm, and begin to change the child's perspective. Teaching children self-hypnosis returns some sense of control and mastery to their lives by enhancing their perception of the controllability of pain. Hypnosis provides them with an active self-management strategy that can enhance their feelings of self-worth and self-esteem, and at the same time reduce their focus on themselves and their pain.

The child's painful experience can be modified. The experienced hypnotherapist will join with the child by pacing and leading her through careful use of language, timing, and tone. The hypnotherapist must reframe the situation and utilize whatever the child brings to the experience so that a paradigm shift results. In keeping with the child's coping style, the therapist must select and use appropriate pain management imagery strategies: dissociation and distraction, direct suggestion, distancing from pain, direct attention to pain, and suggestions for feelings antithetical to pain. Finally, ego-strengthening suggestions and praise should be given for any measure of success.

## Other Uses of Hypnosis

There are many clinical applications for hypnosis in pediatrics. Hypnotherapeutic approaches can be used for children with psychological disorders. Motivated children can learn self-regulatory strategies to help manage aggression and anger. Hypnotherapy may be part of a treatment plan for children with obsessive–compulsive disorder. Hypnosis allows the child to focus on a solution rather than the problem. Ego strengthening enhances confidence and ability to master problems.

Psychological factors can affect asthma. Therefore, teaching children with asthma self-hypnosis can be a useful adjunct to treatment. The symptoms of Irritable Bowel Syndrome can be exacerbated by stress. Hypnotherapy can be combined with medical management to modulate and moderate the symptoms. Children, especially, do not like to be labeled by their disease. Compliance with the medical management of chronic illnesses can be difficult for the child and challenging for the clinician.

Children with cancer can use hypnosis to help themselves with unpleasant procedures and treatment side effects. It is possible for self-hypnosis strategies to enhance immune function and effect the outcome of the disease process. Death is never easy, and the death of a child is certainly tragic. Based on the child's belief system, hypnosis can help him through this traumatic period.

Preparing a child hypnotically for surgery may result in decreased anxiety, a shorter hospital stay, faster recovery, and a decreased need for pain medications. A child's sense of mastery and competency is enhanced. Once the techniques are learned, the child may use them to manage challenges throughout life.

## Summary

The metaphor of "How Harry the Hypno-potamus Got His Name" is a unique and effective way to introduce children to the magic of imagination and hypnosis. Also included in this text is a two-page hand-out that may be duplicated and given to parents to enhance their understanding of hypnotic intervention therapy.

Metaphors can ignite a child's creative imagination. Very young children may not need to figure out the meaning of the metaphor; rather, they immerse themselves in the fanciful tale and become intimately connected to the sensory experience. The child's simplistic and intuitive grasp of situations allows him to be open to the symbolic dimension and diversion of the experience. When the child is fully immersed in the story, his personal internal negative dialogue may be suppressed and new possibilities flourish. The child can make a personal connection with the character's situation or problem.

The techniques embedded in these tales can be used for a variety of mental and physical problems. Many of the techniques can be adapted for children at diverse developmental levels. The goals of these hypnotherapeutic metaphors are altering, re-interpreting and reframing. Above all, the child and the clinician should have fun with them.

# Guide To Using The Tales

Contained within some of the stories are hypnotic scripts. Pacing, leading, cadence, rhythm, and vocal inflections are all important in hypnosis. In the scripted portion of the tales, the words that deserve emphasis in a hypnotic intervention are in bold face type.

The story, "How Harry the Hypno-potamus Got His Name", may be used to introduce a child to the concept of hypnosis and the power of imagination.

The zoo's veterinarian, Dr. Dan, who is skilled in the use of hypnosis, helps Harry learn how to use his imagination when he is worried about getting an immunization. The hippopotamus discovers that he can use similar techniques when he is experiencing pain from a toothache. Tapping into his imagination also helps Harry deal with the anxiety he is feeling about moving to a new place.

This story can be read to a child at the visit when hypnosis is first discussed as an introduction to the modality for both parent and child. Through this story, children realize that hypnosis is not scary, but, like daydreaming, rather enjoyable, and something they are already good at doing.

## Anxiety

The tales of the koala, gazelle, warthog, and turtle concern anxiety, a common pediatric problem. The bat's problems with falling asleep can be related to anxiety. The jaguar, walrus, elephant, otter, and gorilla all have fears. Performance anxiety and mental skills training are the subjects of the stories of the monkeys and the cockatoo.

## Mind–Body Connection
## (Claire Koala)

The story of Claire Koala is a wonderful way to introduce children to the inter-connectedness of mind and body and how, even without their realizing it, their thoughts and feelings can affect them physically. The clinician can suggest that the child extend her arms out from the shoulders. The clinician then pushes gently down on the child's arms. As the child continues to extend her arms, she is asked to think of something sad for a few moments.

The clinician again pushes down on the child's arms with the same amount of force as he used previously. As the child continues to extend her arms, the clinician asks her to think happy thoughts about strength and power. After a few moments of positive thinking, the clinician again gently pushes down on the child's arms. The difference in strength when the child is thinking positive-versus-negative thoughts is usually quite apparent. This is a great way to begin a discussion about how our thoughts can affect our bodies. Claire learns diaphragmatic breathing as an induction technique and relaxation strategy that she can use on her own.

## Anxiety Attacks and Biofeedback
## (Linda Gazelle)

In the story of Linda Gazelle, anxiety is reframed, and the physiology of a panic attack is explained in a way that is developmentally appropriate for a young child. Contained within the tale of Linda is another metaphor concerning the amygdala and the higher centers of the brain. The amygdala is part of the limbic system. The amygdala cannot distinguish between what is real and what is imagined. It is up to the higher cognitive centers in the brain to reason and evaluate the amygdala's automatic reaction.

The clinician teaches the gazelle diaphragmatic breathing by using a yoyo technique that works well for young children. This technique allows the clinician to initially lead and pace, then acknowledge that the child is in complete control.

Cyberphysiology, the self-regulation of physiologic processes, represents the interface of clinical hypnosis and biofeedback. Biofeedback and hypnosis are synergistic and complementary. Cyberphysiology taps into the child's natural drive for self-control and mastery by utilizing the patient's creative and imaginative skills. This metaphor illustrates how they can be cultivated to act as a bridge to therapeutic change.

## Sleep Disorder
## (Brownie Bat)

A child's sleeping problems are frequently the result of anxiety. Brownie Bat is taught progressive muscle relaxation. The suggestion to "pretend to pretend that you are sleeping, and then pretend that you are not pretending" is an example of trance logic. This

metaphor also suggests a technique for getting rid of unwanted or anxious thoughts that interfere with sleep.

## General Anxiety
## (Marlene Worry Warthog)

In this metaphor, a worried warthog is helped to control her anxiety. Her imagination is compared to an elevator that can take her up to wonderful places, or down to someplace she would rather not be. Marlene Worry Warthog learns to create a special trash receptacle for all her "what-if" worries.

## Social Anxiety
## (Shy Sheryll Turtle)

The magic carpet induction contained in this story works well for children of all ages. Empowering the child to be in the driver's seat provides a feeling of safety while encouraging the child to stretch her imagination. Embedded in this tale of Shy Sheryll Turtle are two more metaphors: a rubber band that becomes very useful when it is stretched, and a butterfly that must struggle by itself to emerge from a chrysalis so it can get out and fly free. The story ends with a double bind: success now or success later.

## Needle Phobia
## (Jordan Jaguar)

Children love magic and fantasy. This story demonstrates how clinicians can incorporate magic into their work with children. When rapport needs to be established quickly with a child, sharing a magic trick can be very useful. In this metaphor, Jordan Jaguar is empowered to play a magic trick on his brain. The metaphor contains two inductions that are effective with children. The first one uses a jaguar's tail to describe arm levitation. The second induction involves focusing the child's attention on the movement of a magical feeling, then using that magic as an anesthetic. This story also incorporates a jettison technique and distraction by blowing away the pain.

## Fear of Thunderstorms
## (Oster Otter)

When working hypnotically with children, it is critically important to incorporate special interests and talents that the child possesses or brings with him to the encounter. The otter likes to play and slide; thus, a desensitization metaphor that involves an amusement park ride is contained within the tale of Oster Otter. Seascape, a very effective technique for a variety of disorders, is described in this story. The otter places his worry and fear in the sand, and watches as the ocean waves carry it out to sea. This works well for pain, and is also used in the story of the coatimundi.

## Fear of the Dark and Enclosed Spaces
## (Dabney Gorilla)

The induction technique of coming down a hillside, utilizing the child's favorite sport or mode of transportation, is popular with older children. This metaphor of Dabney Gorilla describes ideomotor signaling and how it may be established. The technique can be useful when working with older children. Younger children generally have no problem talking while in trance, and, in fact, will often have their eyes open, and may be actively moving about.

When working with a fearful child, desensitization and rapport building take time. The clinician must allow the child to set the pace while gently encouraging him forward in the direction he wishes to move. When using desensitization, the clinician slowly moves the child closer to his goal in his imagination. Imagination is stronger than will power. When will power and imagination conflict, imagination will always win out over will. As the child visualizes success, the story offers ego-strengthening suggestions.

## Dental Phobia
## (Elkins Elephant)

Fear of the dentist is the subject of the story of Elkins Elephant, which utilizes distraction through relaxation and mental imagery. The Ericksonian technique of "my friend John" can be helpful when there is resistance to change. The story contains a fishing metaphor about how easy it is to remove a fishhook when the fish is holding still.

## Fear of MRI
## (Valerie Walrus)

During childhood, some individuals may need to have a CT scan or MRI. The equipment may seem frightening, and holding still is difficult. The metaphor of Valerie Walrus offers the child a technique to reframe the procedure into an exciting space ride.

## Performance Anxiety
## (Wark Cockatoo)

This story is about a performing cockatoo who gets nervous when he is to sing in the zoo's bird show. First, he learns belly, or diaphragmatic breathing, an invaluable technique for anyone who experiences anxiety. To prepare for his appearance, Wark Cockatoo visualizes giving his best performance. The clinician suggests that Wark can rewind and improve his singing in his imagination until he gets it just the way he wants it to be. In this metaphor, the performer learns alert hypnosis and the Stein clenched fist technique. Both enable him to power in confidence and displace anxiety.

## Sports Performance
## (Max and Mitch Monkey)

For competitive athletes, having the right mindset is very important. In this story, Mitch Monkey learns which factors in competition he can control, and which ones he can't. He learns techniques for letting go of the things that are not within his control, but could negatively impact his performance. He also learns the importance of positive self-talk. The story illustrates the performance-enhancing technique of programming in success and programming out mistakes.

# Habit Disorders

Many children need help in overcoming their habit disorders. Many of the techniques used in the story of the macaw with trichotillomania are applicable to thumb sucking, nail biting, or scab picking. The relaxation response, which is frequently an integral part of hypnosis, can be very beneficial for children with habit disorders such as a tic (in the tale of Ol'Ness Bunny) or bruxism (in the tale of Voit Zebra). The stories about the meerkat with enuresis and the llama with encopresis both discuss toileting issues.

## Thumb Sucking and Nail Biting
## (Cory and Candy Chimpanzee)

Cory and Candy Chimpanzee have thumb sucking and nail biting habits. This metaphor uses helping hands and visualizing success techniques along with the ego-strengthening which should be a part of every hypnotic encounter. The clinician also suggests the Ericksonian technique of prescribing the symptom. Although this may initially seem counterproductive, the technique helps children to be more mindful of their habits, and to realize that they do have control. Many habit disorders are exacerbated by anxiety or stress. It is always beneficial for a child to learn to relax by using her imagination.

## Trichotillomania
## (Molly Macaw)

Molly Macaw pulls out her feathers until she learns to imagine a friend gently pushing her beak away from her plumage whenever she starts plucking. Stop sign imagery and turning down the triggers are used to treat Molly Macaw's trichotillomania. When working with a child who has a disfiguring habit disorder, a mirroring technique can be helpful. The child visualizes the hair, the skin, or the nails she wishes to have.

## Tic Disorder
### (Ol'Ness Bunny)

In the story of Ol'Ness, the rabbit with a tic disorder learns progressive muscle relaxation, beginning far away from the tic, to help control her habit. This tale describes the techniques of saving the tic until later, displacing the tic, and turning down the twitch switch. Ol'Ness Bunny learns to prolong the time between the urge to tic and the tic by visualizing a yellow light, then stopping it with a red light.

Within the story is a metaphor of descending a mountain. The winds are blowing the leaves on the trees at the top of the mountain. As Ol'Ness imagines that she is coming down the mountain, the wind calms and the leaves become still.

## Bruxism
### (Voit Zebra)

For the zebra with bruxism, progressive relaxation begins far away from his teeth. Strongly kinesthetic guided imagery is helpful. The story of Voit Zebra presents a metaphor for creating relaxed, gentle space in the mouth.

## Enuresis
### (Sugar Man Meerkat)

Enuresis is a developmental or maturational variant, an accidental habit that becomes stuck, or inadvertently perpetuated. Nocturnal enuresis is a common pediatric problem that can have significant negative social implications. In this metaphor, the problem, which can seem so all-encompassing and overwhelming to a child, is reframed as manageable. The physiology is explained in a developmentally appropriate way, and the clinician joins with the child so they can work together as a team to solve the problem. Sugar Man Meerkat is able to overcome his habit by assuming ownership of the problem and understanding how his body and mind work together. The meerkat programs his brain for dry nights, recites a mantra, and visualizes success. Self-monitoring is important, because success begets success.

## Encopresis
### (Lonnie Llama)

The approach to children with encopresis is both physical and psychological, and includes metaphorical approaches about putting things where they need to go. Mastery metaphors, and ego strengthening are important. Relaxing, letting go, and special imagery were helpful techniques for Lonnie Llama when combined with regular toileting routines, diet, and medication.

# Pain

The three tales about animals in pain deal with acute, chronic, and recurring pain.

## Acute Injury
### (Davey Manatee)

When Davey Manatee suffers an acute injury, he is already in an altered state of focused absorption. Reframing the injury and the bleeding begins immediately. Practicing "ouch" is both confusional and empowering. It is likely that no one has ever asked Davey to yell louder. He is also given the suggestion that he can control the size "ouch" that he needs. The story describes distraction that incorporates multiple senses, as well as ego-strengthening, a key ingredient in any hypnotic encounter. Children want to know what is happening to them. In this metaphor, Davey is encouraged to ask questions about the procedure and his surroundings.

## Chronic Pain
### (Handel Tapir)

The tale of Handel Tapir is about chronic pain. The induction technique of a magnetic force pulling fingers closer together can be used with both children and adults. Hypnosis is a gift that you give yourself. Handel receives a present containing a comfort cloak. This is a variation of glove anesthesia for the entire body. Children who are fans of Harry Potter will have no trouble imagining a magical cloak. The side-by-side screen technique can be adapted to many problems. Giving the child the remote controls clearly places control in his hands. This metaphor also incorporates a time-distortion technique.

For some patients with chronic pain, secondary gain can be a powerful motivator to maintain the pain. Asking the question, "Is there anything about the pain that you will miss when it is gone?" can be very telling. It is always important to pay special attention to the use of language, such as using the word "when" instead of "if," and placing pain in the past tense; e.g. "the pain you used to have." Handel also uses future projection to visualize life being better without the pain. "I'm not sure if it will be tomorrow or next week that . . ." is a double bind. The hypnotherapist is suggesting success or success, tomorrow or next week.

## Headaches
### (Julie Giraffe)

Self-regulatory strategies can be extraordinarily helpful for children with headaches. The most effective coping strategies for a child to manage pain will vary depending on whether he is an avoider or an attender. Avoiders find distraction techniques quite helpful. Attenders often do better altering the perception. Both strategies are included in the story of Julie Giraffe. The giraffe learns that she can take a vacation from her headache by going somewhere wonderful in her imagination, or stay where she is and send the headache away.

Moving the headache to a place on her body where it is less bothersome, while at the same time changing the nature of the discomfort, is often helpful for attenders. Another technique included in the metaphor is to give the headache a color and watch it change to the color of comfort. This tale also illustrates the technique of giving the pain a number to correspond to its intensity, and then dialing the number down. Julie's pain is reframed as a signal.

## Other Uses of Hypnosis

The remaining stories are about other ways hypnosis can be used in pediatrics. Two metaphors address behavioral techniques for use with anger management and obsessive-compulsive disorder. There are also metaphors for such chronic illnesses as asthma, diabetes, epilepsy, and irritable bowel.

Children coping with cancer, and the helpful and healthful effects of humor, are the subjects of the tale of the sloth. A metaphor for terminally ill children is also included, and a helpful script for the child facing surgery.

The final two stories deal with the diversity of personal characteristics, traits, and talents, and the many varied but loving families that children come from.

## Anger Management
### (Milton Cheetah)

Unfortunately, there are many children who can relate to the story of Milton, who is treated badly by people who were supposed to care for him. The cheetah learns that anger is natural and normal, but it can be expressed in detrimental ways. Milton learns diaphragmatic, or belly, breathing, and experiences the calming effects of relaxation and mental imagery. A jettison technique helps him to get rid of angry feelings.

The clinician can ask the child to remember a time in the past when he was angry and reacted poorly, and review it in slow motion. The child can then re-wind and stop the anger before it starts, and then re-write it, or give that past memory a new ending. Ego strengthening suggestions are given as the child is able to imagine improved behavior and control.

## Obsessive–Compulsive Disorder
### (Norma and Phil Beaver)

In this metaphor of Norma and Phil Beaver, the role of a psychologist is introduced. Obsessive–compulsive behavior seems to have overtaken the beaver's life. When this is reframed, the beaver realizes that there are times when the repetitive behavior and the obsessive thoughts are not always present. Relaxation and mental imagery, along with time distortion, increase the times of having fun, and decrease the time of obsessive–compulsive activities.

## Irritable Bowel Syndrome (IBS)
### (Olafur Ostrich)

Many children with IBS have discovered that stress and anxiety can aggravate their symptoms. Relaxation and mental imagery can be very helpful. Olafur Ostrich imagines a cone of his favorite ice cream melting, and coating his intestines with cool comfort. The clinician suggests that only pleasant sensations can go through, and offers the kinesthetic image of the natural, gentle rhythm of the ocean. The ostrich finds a seashell on the beach and notices how cool, smooth, and pink the inside of the shell is.

The clinician suggests that Olafur will see a shelter safe from any storm. There is a dimmer switch to block out uncomfortable sensations. As the dimmer switch is dialed down, the inside of the shelter becomes pleasantly pink. The clinician suggests that Olafur can return to this place of comfort at any time, because it is a place that is always within him. The idea is very empowering.

An example of a reinforcer, using trance logic, is also demonstrated in this tale. The ostrich is given the suggestion that his eyes are glued shut. When he is convinced that they are successfully glued shut, the clinician suggests that he try to open them.

## Asthma
### *(Spiegel Eagle)*

Respiratory distress can be terrifying. The symptoms can be exacerbated by the increasing anxiety of breathlessness. The calming effect of hypnosis can be very therapeutic. Spiegel Eagle visualizes a comfortable time without wheezing. The eagle imagines his airways relaxing and expanding, and air flowing easily in and out. Using his imagination, he sees and feels his medicine working, and a Pacman-type creature ridding his lungs of mucous. Hypnosis, used as an adjunctive therapy in the treatment of asthma, may increase the effectiveness of medication and thus decrease the amounts needed.

## Diabetes and Epilepsy
### *(Mutter Moose and Elgan Elk)*

It is frequently difficult for a child with a chronic condition that requires daily medical management to be compliant. In this metaphor, Mutter Moose and Elgan Elk, a moose with diabetes and an elk with epilepsy, learn that although they have a disease, the disease doesn't have to have them. Mutter and Elgan can take the "IC" out of diabetic and epileptic when they take care of themselves.

## Leukemia
### *(Lazarus Sloth)*

Laughter is very therapeutic; it releases endorphins, the body's natural opiates. Lazarus Sloth has leukemia. Lazarus has a great sense of humor, and is encouraged to utilize this resource to enhance health and healing. In this metaphor, the concept of

the pain switch is introduced, along with a speed-o-scope that is capable of speeding up or slowing down time perception.

Psychoneuroimmunology refers to the neuroendocrine, neurochemical and neuroanatomical links to the immune system; it is intentional immunomodulation. With hypnosis, the sloth is able to mobilize intrinsic healing and immunologic stimulation directed against his malignancy.

Lazarus imagines each of his chemotherapy medications working, and his body successfully defeating the disease. He learns an effective therapeutic technique—future projection—and visualizes a time when his body is healed and well. Then he uses an affect bridge to bring those good feelings back to the present.

## Terminal Illness
### *(Lynch Coatimundi)*

Lynch Coatimundi, has a fatal illness. By alleviating the suffering and anxiety of the disease process and its treatment, hypnotherapy can be very advantageous for the child with a terminal condition. It can help the child prepare for death and feel more in control of the dying process. Engaging the child with fantasy can hasten the time of discomfort, and lift the spirits of a depressed child.

For many people, an ocean beach is a relaxing, peaceful place. Placing pain, anxieties, and worries in a pile of sand, and suggesting that a change is taking place, arouses the child's curiosity. He envisions the tide changing, and the waves taking the worries out to sea as the pile gets smaller and smaller with each soothing wave. The technique can be adapted to many different emotional and physical problems. The child with trichotillomania could put the urge to pull her hair in a pile of seashore sand. When the urge to pull that is contained in that pile is all washed out to sea, the sand becomes smooth, and the beach grows lush with sea lavender and beach grass.

Lynch reviews tender memories of a deceased grandmother and a doll that brought him comfort. He visualizes death calmly and peacefully, surrounded by familiar, loving relatives to ease his transition into whatever follows life. Children sometimes accept the inevitability of their death before their parents do, and need to talk about their concerns, wishes and fears with a trusting, nurturing adult.

## Surgery
## (Pam Penguin)

Surgery can be a painful and anxiety provoking experience, especially for children. With hypnosis, that experience can be reframed. The safety and security of home rituals and routines are totally disrupted when a child is hospitalized and has surgery. Preparing a child hypnotically for surgery and hospitalization can empower her to do what she needs to do to increase her level of comfort. Preoperative interruptions are used for fractionation.

The clinician suggests that the surgical patient pay attention only to the voice speaking to her directly. The hypnosis reinforces the child's feelings of safety, comfort and relaxation, and reassures her that the nurses and doctors will take good care of her. Suggestions for constricting blood flow to the operative area are given in a developmentally appropriate way.

Pam Penguin imagines being completely recovered and feeling good. The potentially painful postoperative period is reframed as one of healing and mending. To prevent any postoperative

vomiting, the suggestion is given that food travels only in one direction.

If a clinician skilled in hypnosis is not available to physically accompany the child through the surgical procedure, a tape recording can be used to prepare her in the days before surgery. Later, it can be used in the preoperative area, and during the surgery.

## Family Constellations

Today, the majority of children no longer grow up in a loving, two-parent household where the father works and the mother stays home to care for the children and the house. The diversity of what makes up a family is the subject of this metaphor. The animals discuss whether or not they grew up with two parents, or with a single parent. Some animals never knew both of their parents, or were raised by surrogates. They discover that love is the unifying factor of all their differing families.

## Appreciating Diversity
## (It Makes a World of Difference)

In this metaphor about diversity, all of the animals envy characteristics possessed by other animals. Each is made to feel unique, and endowed with special gifts and talents.

17

# References

## Books and Videotapes

Belnap, Martha. *Taming Your Dragons*. Boulder, CO: The Village Printer, 1986.

Belnap, Martha. *Taming More Dragons*. Boulder, CO: The Village Printer, 1994.

Both of these books are collections of creative relaxation activities for children. They include breathing exercises, imagery experiences, and playful activities that help children learn skills that help them identify their own moods and understand the importance of self-control and relaxation.

Burton, John, and Bodenhamer, Bob. *Hypnotic Language, Its Structure and Use*. Carmarthen, Wales, UK: Crown House Publishing, 2000.

This book is a wonderful resource for beginning clinicians seeking to learn the language of trance, or for experienced clinicians to enhance their language of healing. With strong backgrounds in neurolinguistic programming, the authors provide the reader with insight into the magic of words. The book provides trance scripts and creative ways to induce cognitive change.

Hammond, D.C. (Ed.) *Handbook of Hypnotic Suggestions and Metaphors*. New York: W.W. Norton & Co., 1990.

"The big red book", indispensable for anyone who utilizes hypnosis in clinical practice, covers the broad range of uses for hypnosis in medicine, dentistry, and psychology. The contributing authors, who are the best of the best in their field, create a practical, comprehensive desktop reference of "how to" suggestions for clinicians to employ with their patients.

Hilgard, J.R., and LeBaron, S. *Hypnotherapy of Pain in Children with Cancer*. Los Altos, CA: William Kaufman, Inc., 1984.

A comprehensive study of the effects of hypnosis on reducing pain and anxiety in children with cancer. While presenting the results of extensive research, the authors offer developmentally appropriate tools and techniques for both professionals and the parents of children with cancer.

Hunter, Marlene. *Creative Scripts for Hypnotherapy*. New York: Brunner-Routledge, 1994.

This book is a treasure, a collection of this gifted clinician's favorite hypnotic techniques and approaches. In addition to a section with scripts for children, there are techniques for pain relief, psychosomatic disorders, fears, phobias, habit disorders and general ego-strengthening approaches. It is an incredibly valuable and insightful handbook of creative scripts.

Klein, Nancy. *Healing Images for Children*. Watertown, WI: Inner Coaching, 2001.

With insight drawn from her personal experience with cancer, the author combines engaging pictures and stories to help children find their own strategies for coping and healing. The book is a wonderful resource for children and their caregivers as they confront cancer or some other serious medical condition. Companion CDs, activity books, and relaxation kits are also available from the author.

Kuttner, Leora. *No Fears, No Tears: Children with Cancer Coping with Pain*. Vancouver, Canada: Canadian Cancer Society, 1986.

Dr. Kuttner is a clinical psychologist who specializes in childhood pain management. This thirty minute videotape and manual showcases her work with seriously ill children. Her skilled and gentle manner and the effective techniques she employs are captured on film..

Kuttner, Leora. *No Fears, No Tears: 13 Years Later*. Vancouver, Canada: Canadian Cancer Society, 1999.

This thirty minute videotape and manual follows the children who appeared on the video "*No Fears, No Tears*" thirteen years later. The children discuss how hypnosis helped them help themselves not only with their illness but with life.

Kuttner, Leora. *A Child in Pain: How to Help, What to Do*. Washington: Hartley & Marks, 1996.

A resource book for parents and professionals working with children. The book teaches its readers how to help children of different ages through life's difficult and painful moments.

Mills, Joyce C., and Crowley, Richard J. *Therapeutic Metaphors for Children and The Child Within*. New York: Brunner/Mazel, 1986.

The authors describe their own applications of Ericksonian approaches to pediatric problems, and provide a framework for understanding the potency of metaphor in blending right and left brain functions. Mills and Crowley also discuss the process of creating therapeutic metaphors to stimulate each person's unique internal resources.

Olness, K. and Kohen, D.P. *Hypnosis and Hypnotherapy with Children* (Third Edition). New York: Guilford Publications, Inc., 1996.

Written by two eminent clinicians, the third edition is a comprehensive guide to pediatric hypnosis that begins with a historical perspective and continues with a review of the literature and its clinical applications. Olness and Kohen provide specific techniques for a variety of pediatric problems, along with examples of actual cases. The book is an indispensable resource for the clinician who works hypnotically with children.

Sugarman, Lawrence. "Imaginative Medicine." Rochester, NY: Pulse Productions, 1997.

Dr. Sugarman, a general pediatrician, created this 70-minute videotape and learning guide as a practical, in-depth introduction to mind–body methods in pediatrics. The documentary demonstrates hypnotic techniques that are used in a pediatric office daily, and shows how the techniques comfort children during medical examinations and procedures, and also help them to manage stress as they cope with chronic illness. The video includes personal reports from young people who have utilized self-regulatory strategies to help themselves.

Wester, William C., and O'Grady, Donald. *Clinical Hypnosis with Children*. New York: Brunner/Mazel, 1991.

Sixteen experts in the field of hypnosis contributed chapters to this text. The book begins with an overview of hypnosis in pediatrics. Subsequent chapters discuss psychological and medical applications of hypnosis in working with children.

## Journal Articles

Culbert, T., Reaney, J., and Kohen, D.P. "Cyberphysiologic Strategies in Children: The Biofeedback-Hypnosis Interface." *The International Journal of Clinical and Experimental Hypnosis*, 1994.

Edwards, S.D., and Van Der Spuy, H.I.J. "Hypnotherapy as a Treatment for Enuresis." *Journal of Child Psychology and Psychiatry*, 26, 1985: 161–170.

Gardner, G.G. "Childhood, Death, and Human Dignity: Hypnotherapy for David." *International Journal of Clinical and Experimental Hypnosis*, 24, 1976: 122–139.

Gardner, G.G. "Hypnotherapy in the Management of Childhood Habit Disorders." *Journal of Pediatrics*, 92, 1978: 834.

Jacknow, D.S., Tschann, J.M., Link, M.P., and Boyce, W.T. "Hypnosis in the Prevention of Chemotherapy-Related Nausea and Vomiting in Children: A Prospective Study." *Journal of Developmental and Behavioral Pediatric*, 15, 4, 1994: 258–264.

Kohen, D.P., Olness, K.N., Colwell, S., and Heimel, A. "The use of Relaxation/Mental Imagery (Self-Hypnosis) in the Management of 505 Pediatric Behavioral Encounters." *Journal of Developmental and Behavioral Pediatrics*, 1, 5, 1984: 21–25.

Kohen, D.P. "Applications of Relaxation/Mental Imagery (Self-Hypnosis) in Pediatric Emergencies." *International Journal of Clinical and Experimental Hypnosis*, 34, 4, 1986: 283–294.

Kohen, D.P. "Applications of Relaxation and Mental Imagery (Self-Hypnosis) for Habit Problems." *Pediatric Annals*, 20, 3, 1991: 136–144.

Kohen, D.P., and Olness, K.N. "Self-Regulation Therapy: Helping Children to Help Themselves." *Ambulatory Child Health: Journal of General and Community Pediatrics*, 2, 1996: 43–58.

Kohen, D.P., and Wynne, E. "Applying Hypnosis in a Preschool Family Asthma Education Program: Uses of Storytelling, Imagery and Relaxation." *American Journal of Clinical Hypnosis*, 39, 3, 1997: 2–14.

Kohen, D.P. "Hypnosis in the Treatment of Asthma." *The Integrative Medicine Consult*, 2, 2000: 61–62.

Kuttner, Leora. "Favorite Stories: A Hypnotic Pain Reduction Technique for Children in Acute Pain." *American Journal of Clinical Hypnosis*, 30, 1988: 289–295.

LaBaw, W.L., Holton, C., Tewell, K., and Eccles, D. "The Use of Self-Hypnosis by Children with Cancer." *American Journal of Clinical Hypnosis*, 17, 1975: 233–238.

Olness, K. " Imagery (Self-Hypnosis) as Adjunct Therapy in Childhood Cancer: Clinical Experience With 25 Patients." *American Journal of Pediatric Hematology/Oncology*, 3, 1981: 313–321.

Olness, K. "The Use of Self-Hypnosis in the Treatment of Childhood Nocturnal Enuresis." *Clinical Pediatrics*, 14, 1975: 273–279.

Olness, K., MacDonald, J., and Uden, D. "Prospective Study Comparing Propranalol Placebo and Hypnosis in Management of Juvenile Migraine." *Pediatrics*, 79, 4, 1987: 593–597.

Sperry R. "Hemispheric disconnection and unity of conscious awareness." *American Psychologist*, 23, 1968: 723–733.

Sugarman, L.I. "Hypnosis: Teaching Children Self-Regulation." *Pediatrics in Review*, 17, 1, 1996: 5–11.

Thomson, Linda. "A Project to Change the Attitudes, Beliefs and Practices of Health Professionals Concerning Hypnosis." *American Journal of Hypnosis*, 46, 1, 2002: 31–44.

Thomson, Linda. "Hypnosis for Habit Disorders." *Advance for Nurse Practitioners*, 10, 7, 2002: 59–62.

# *Information about Hypnosis for Parents*

**Hypnosis is about learning what you didn't know you knew and controlling what you didn't know you could . . . using your mind . . . daydreaming on purpose . . . thinking to help yourself . . . learning how to work to control your mind . . .**

## What is Hypnosis?

Hypnosis is a very old healing modality, a safe, gentle, and effective way to heal, reduce stress, relieve pain, and effect changes in one's life. Hypnosis is a state of mind similar to experiencing a pleasant daydream. People in a hypnotic trance may look like they are asleep, but they are actually relaxed, concentrating, and using their imagination.

If a hypnotherapist is involved, she acts as a coach or facilitator, guiding the person's daydream. The individual patient controls entering and exiting this relaxed state of consciousness. An individual can learn self-hypnosis so he can enter that state of comfort and increased self-control at any time for his own benefit. Learning self-hypnosis is a valuable lifelong skill that is good for the body, mind and spirit.

## What is Hypnotherapy?

When a properly trained and credentialed health care professional uses hypnosis as a part of treatment, it is called hypnotherapy. Hypnotherapy is a practical way of helping people manage physical and psychological problems. The hypnotherapist uses relaxation, focused guided imagery, suggestions, and therapeutic metaphors to build self-control over physical and emotional problems.

Contrary to how hypnosis may be portrayed in the movies and on television, the hypnotherapist does not control the individual's behavior. Stage hypnotists take advantage of willing volunteers for the purpose of entertainment. This powerful and personal skill is a gift too valuable for just this purpose. Hypnosis is a state of intense self-control. The therapist may use helpful words to suggest ways to feel, understand, or behave, but she cannot control the person in hypnosis. Although hypnosis makes it easier for people to experience therapeutic suggestions, it does not force them to have these experiences.

**All hypnosis is self-hypnosis that can be used for one's own benefit.**

*Reprinted with permission from Harry the Hypno-potamus: Metaphorical Tales for the Treatment of Children, by Linda Thomson © Crown House Publishing Limited, 2005*

## What are the Risks of Hypnotherapy?

When used correctly, there are no risks to hypnotherapy, nor any adverse effects. The technique increases one's ability to control symptoms. The brain is incredibly powerful, and contains priceless resources which can be mobilized for personal growth and healing. Hypnosis helps the individual to use his own imagination to tap into his inner strengths and resources. **Hypnosis should only be used as part of a treatment plan for a specific problem after a careful evaluation by a trained health professional.**

## Why Use Hypnotherapy?

Hypnotherapy has been used successfully to treat pain, anxiety, fears, phobias, pain, asthma, bedwetting, stool-withholding, nervous tics, smoking, obesity and many other problems. **The value of hypnosis goes beyond its ability to help with these ailments**. Increasing one's ability to control symptoms through hypnosis can strengthen confidence and mastery. Personal success in self-hypnosis increases self-esteem. Self-hypnosis is a skill that increases with practice. The techniques can be used to meet new challenges throughout life.

**For more information about the use of
hypnosis with children contact:**

American Society of Clinical Hypnosis
140 N. Bloomingdale Road
Bloomingdale, Illinois 60108-1017
www.asch.net
Phone: 630-980-4740
Fax: 630-351-8490
Email: info@asch.net

Society for Developmental and Behavioral Pediatrics
17000 Commerce Parkway, Suite C
Mt. Laurel, New Jersey 08054
www.sdbp.org
Phone: 856-439-0500
Fax: 856-439-0525
Email: sdbp@ahint.com

*Reprinted with permission from Harry the Hypno-potamus: Metaphorical Tales for the Treatment of Children, by Linda Thomson © Crown House Publishing Limited, 2005*

# The Tales For Children

# How Harry the Hypno-potamus Got His Name

Harry is a hippopotamus. He lives at the Ashland Zoo. Harry has a wonderful imagination.

Harry's very favorite place is a big mud puddle beside his home. He loves to hide there and pretend he is a submarine. When he is all covered up with mud, Harry feels invisible to all the visitors who come to the zoo.

Dr. Dan is the veterinarian who takes care of all the animals. One day he came to give Harry an immunization shot so he wouldn't get sick. Harry was scared because he didn't like needles.

"I know what a great imagination you have," said Dr. Dan. "I'm going to show you how to use your imagination so the shot won't bother you."

Harry was intrigued. "Could you show me right now?" he asked.

"Of course," said Dr. Dan. "Close your eyes and imagine you are in your favorite place."

Harry closed his eyes. "I'm in my mud puddle," he said happily.

"Next," said Dr. Dan, "imagine that you are hiding in the mud. Nobody can see you. You are safe and secure."

Harry imagined that he was all covered up with mud. The soft, cool mud felt good against his skin. He felt very relaxed.

"Now, take a deep breath," said Dr. Dan. "Imagine that you are blowing bubbles in the mud."

Harry giggled and took a deep breath. He pretended to blow bubbles. He was having so much fun thinking about his mud puddle that he hardly noticed the little pinch when the needle poked him.

One day Harry had a very bad toothache. Dr. Dan came to see him.

"Remember how your terrific imagination helped you when I came to give you the immunization shot?"

"But my tooth really hurts," said Harry.

Dr. Dan nodded sympathetically. "Using your imagination may help it to hurt less," he said.

Harry took a deep breath. "I'm ready."

"Close your eyes and imagine you are having lots of fun," said Dr. Dan.

Harry smiled. "When I was a little hippo," he said, "my Daddy told me stories about Africa. The mud puddles there are huge, so lots of hippos can get in the mud together."

Harry closed his eyes and imagined that he was in a giant mud puddle in Africa. Lots of hippos were in the mud with him, splashing and blowing bubbles. He was so busy thinking about that mud puddle that he almost forgot all about his toothache.

One day, when Harry was playing in his mud puddle, his friend Pam Penguin waddled up to him, flapping her wings in excitement.

"We're moving!" she cried. "The zoo is building a new and better place for us all to live."

"Moving!" Harry felt sick to his stomach. He wanted everything to remain the same. He liked the familiar, comfortable place he had with his very own mud puddle. Harry wasn't sure that he wanted a new home. He felt scared.

Then Harry remembered how Dr. Dan had taught him to use his imagination to control his thoughts and feelings.

"I call it hypnosis," said Dr. Dan. "It's all about learning what you didn't know you knew. It's thinking to help yourself."

Harry imagined what his new home would be like. Hippos can't see very well, but they have a wonderful sense of smell. Harry imagined what his new home would smell like. He imagined how soft and cool his new mud puddle would be. The mud puddle made him feel safe and secure, just like the old one did. Pretending and thinking about his new home helped Harry to not feel so scared on moving day.

When the zoo truck brought Harry to his new home, Dr. Dan was there to welcome him.

"I'm so proud of you!" he told Harry. "You are so good at using hypnosis to help yourself, I brought you a new sign that I made for your new home. The sign said:

**"HARRY, THE HYPNO-POTAMUS"**

# Claire Koala

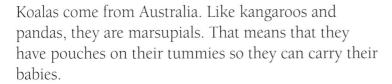

Koalas come from Australia. Like kangaroos and pandas, they are marsupials. That means that they have pouches on their tummies so they can carry their babies.

When Claire Koala was born at the Ashland Zoo, she was very tiny, not much longer than your finger. She was born blind, and she had no hair. She crawled into her mother's pouch where she could get food and stay safe and warm. For six months, Claire snuggled in her mother's pouch, with her forehead resting on her mother's tummy, growing bigger and stronger day by day. Finally, she scrambled out of her mother's pouch.

During the day, the little koala clung to her mother's back while the big koala climbed high in the air, to the very tops of the eucalyptus trees. There Claire and her mother spent the day eating the tender eucalyptus leaves. At night Claire climbed back into her mother's pouch to sleep.

When Claire was fully grown she would be a little over two feet tall. She would be too big to fit inside her mother's pouch. It was cozy in that pouch, snuggled

against her mother. Claire wasn't sure that she would like it when she got too big to crawl back in at night.

Claire's parents argued a lot and that made her sad. The little koala worried about everything. "What if I can't find Mommy in the eucalyptus leaves?" she whispered to herself. "What if all the eucalyptus trees burn down in a fire and I have nothing to eat?" (Koalas eat only eucalyptus leaves.) "What if I'm climbing on a eucalyptus tree all by myself and I slip and fall down out of the tree?"

All of these feelings and worries made Claire feel frightened and scared.

Some of the other koalas picked on Claire because she liked to stay close to her mother. "Scardey–cat! Baby!" they would call when they saw Claire clinging to her motther's back. When the other koalas made fun of her, Claire would get a bad tummy ache.

"You're just faking it," one of Claire's older brothers told her. "You don't really have a stomach ache; you just want to stay in Mommy's pouch!"

Claire began to cry. She knew that she wasn't making it up. Her tummy really did hurt.

"I'm going to call Dr. Dan," Claire's mother said. Dr. Dan was the zoo's veterinarian.

When they got to Dr. Dan's office, the veterinarian said to Claire, "Tell me all about those tummy aches."

Claire told Dr. Dan about how her tummy would hurt whenever she got worried. Dr. Dan talked to Claire for a long time about her tummy aches. Afterward, he checked her over very carefully.

"Your mind and body are all connected, " said Dr. Dan. "They talk to each other all the time. When your stomach growls, that is your tummy talking to your brain. It's saying, 'I'm hungry, please feed me.' When you get goose bumps, that's your body telling your brain that you are cold. It works in the other direction too. Your brain talks to your body all day long. Would you like me to show you how it works?"

Claire nodded, and Dr. Dan lifted her into a eucalyptus tree.

"Hang onto a branch, Claire," he said. Gently he pushed the branch back and forth. "Close your eyes and think about something sad or scary."

As Claire thought about some of the things that worried her, Dr. Dan once again began to move the branch. Claire almost fell off. Her strength seemed to have disappeared.

"Now close your eyes and think about something wonderful," said Dr. Dan.

Claire imagined that she was playing with the other koalas. Everyone was laughing and having fun. Nobody was making fun of her.

"Think about what a good koala you are," said Dr. Dan. "Think about how you are smart and strong."

Claire immediately felt stronger. When Dr. Dan swung the branch even harder, Claire hung on with new strength and vigor.

"Hmmmm," said Dr. Dan. "You were able to change the strength in your muscles just by changing what you were thinking about. When you are thinking about your worries and problems, I wonder what that does to the muscles in your tummy? Hmmmm. I wonder how wonderful it will be for you when you can make your tummy feel better all by yourself, when you use the special powers and abilities of your own mind to help yourself, enjoying that sense of control you have over your body."

"We can begin right now," Dr. Dan continued. "I'll show you how to do belly breathing."

"Belly breathing! What's that?" asked Claire.

"It's a way of taking very deep breaths," answered Dr. Dan. "Those deep breaths can help to make your tummy feel more relaxed. The first thing you do is put your hand right in the middle of your tummy where your belly button would be if you had one."

Claire giggled and followed Dr. Dan's directions.

"Next," said Dr. Dan, "take in a deep breath, and instead of lifting your shoulders, use that breath to lift your tummy up."

Claire's tummy rose up just like a balloon inflating.

"When you let all your breath out," said Dr. Dan, "notice how you can **let go** of a little tension. Breathe in **comfort** and breathe out stress. Breathe in **relaxation** and breathe out tension. Let every breath take you **deeper** and **deeper**, even **more** relaxed, even **more** comfortable; just breathing will do that."

Claire noticed how all her muscles felt even more **relaxed** and **comfortable** with every breath she took. It made her whole body feel good.

"Breathe in **self-confidence** and breathe out uncertainty," said Dr. Dan. "Breathe in **self-esteem** and breathe out self-doubt."

In and out, in and out, breathed Claire. She drew in self-confidence and breathed out uncertainty. She breathed in self-esteem and breathed out self-doubt.

In and out came the breath into Claire's belly. Her tummy rose up and down with every breath. Claire continued to practice her belly breathing, letting go of her tension and worries. She breathed in self-confidence.

"Imagine that you are in a boat on a very large lake," said Dr. Dan. "At first, the water is rough. It is rocking the boat. Gradually, the boat rocks **less** and **less** as the water in the lake gets **smoother** and **smoother**, and even more **calm**, where nothing needs to bother or disturb you."

Claire noticed with interest how her tummy no longer bothered her. That night, she was able to drift off to sleep outside of her mother's pouch dreaming of eucalyptus trees.

# Linda Gazelle

Linda was a Thomson gazelle. The name "gazelle" comes from an Arabic word that means "affectionate." She was gentle and beautiful, with large, soft, black eyes.

Like all of her relatives in the antelope family, Linda was slender and graceful, like a deer. Her round, black horns were bumpy, like a tall string of wooden beads piled one on top of the other. Her coat was smooth and brown, like a deer's. The fur on her belly was white, and separated from the rest of her coat by a stripe of dark fur. Linda came to the Ashland Zoo from the plains and grasslands of Africa. She liked to graze on berries, plants, and leaves.

Gazelles have keen noses for smelling the scents of other animals; especially animals that want to eat them. One of the animals that likes to hunt gazelles is the cheetah. Gazelles can run fast, but these big, spotted cats can run even faster.

Even though Linda was perfectly safe in her area at the Ashland Zoo, she could smell Milton, the cheetah, and hear the frightful sounds he made. Every evening, as the sun was setting and the darkness deepening,

Linda began to get nervous. She was afraid of Milton's roar, which came with the night. Even after Milton learned how to control his temper and no longer roared at night, Linda still got scared as the daylight disappeared.

Sometimes, the gazelle's heart would begin to beat very fast. She got dizzy, and she felt like she couldn't breathe. Dr. Dan said that Linda was having an anxiety, or panic, attack.

"Some anxiety is a good thing," Dr. Dan explained. "If you were on the plains of Africa, and you heard the sound of a cheetah, you would need to run very fast to escape being caught. A gland in your body would send out a messenger, called "adrenalin," to all parts of your body. Adrenalin takes the message to your legs to be strong. It tells your heart to beat fast, so that you can run away from the cheetah; that's a very good thing."

Although Linda was safe at the zoo, thinking about the cheetah, or watching the sun set and the sky get dark could send the adrenalin rushing through her body, even when she was in no danger of being chased. As her heart beat faster, the gazelle felt more scared. The

fear made her body produce even more adrenalin. The additional adrenalin made her heart beat faster still. Linda's panic attack was like a snowball rolling down a hill, going faster and faster, and getting bigger and bigger.

Dr. Dan told a story to Linda about the security guard at the zoo: "Her name is Amy G. Dala. In her office there are many TV screens that monitor all areas of the Ashland Zoo. When something looks suspicious, it is Amy G. Dala's job to sound the alarm. It is not her job to figure out if the danger is real, or only imagined; that is Mr. Grey Matter's responsibility.

"When Mr. Grey Matter was just beginning to work at the zoo, he used to panic every time Amy G. Dala set off the alarm. After a while, though, Mr. Grey Matter learned some ways that helped him not get so worried, excited, and anxious every time that Amy G. Dala sounded the alarm."

Dr. Dan asked Linda if she would like to meet Becky, a very special nurse practitioner. Becky helped patients to help themselves with biofeedback.

"Biofeedback is like a video game for the body," Becky explained.

Linda liked Becky; she had had all sorts of neat stuff to play with.

Becky taught Linda "yoyo breathing." Linda stretched out on her back, then Becky held out her hand about a foot above Linda's soft, white belly.

"Your belly is like a yoyo," Becky suggested, "and I am holding the imaginary string."

As Becky lifted her hand up, Linda took a deep breath way down deep into her belly, and watched her belly rise. As Becky slowly lowered her hand, Linda exhaled. Becky lifted her hand again, and the yoyo of Linda's tummy rose with a deep, relaxing breath. Each time Linda exhaled, she noticed that she was letting go of a little more tension. Breathing slowly and deeply allowed each breath she took to take her deeper and deeper relaxed. When Becky cut the imaginary string on the yoyo, Linda noticed with pride how her tummy continued to slowly rise and fall in comfort, all by itself.

Becky laid some special patches on Linda's shoulders and legs. The patches were connected by wires to a computer that measured and recorded how tight Linda's muscles got when she tightened them, and how loose they got as she relaxed. Becky then asked Linda to tighten as many muscles as she could. Linda watched as the lines on the computer soared up. When she relaxed her muscles, the lines on the

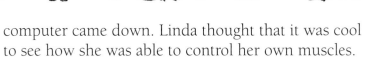

computer came down. Linda thought that it was cool to see how she was able to control her own muscles.

Becky then suggested, "Go back and notice what happens to your breathing when your muscles are tight."

Linda had a hard time doing her yoyo breathing. When she relaxed her muscles, yoyo breathing was easy. As Linda breathed slower and deeper, she saw and felt how her muscles relaxed, and the lines on the computer changed.

After that, Becky did something different with the computer. She put up a screen called a "kaleidoscope." The kaleidoscope had many, many colored lines. Becky asked Linda to tighten all her muscles. Linda did, and all the lines twisted together in a tight shape. Then, as Linda relaxed, the lines unwound and disappeared.

"Now," Becky said, "put your right front hoof on this button. The button is a special sensor that is connected to the computer. It measures the temperature of your hoof. While your foot is on the sensor, think about something that is fun."

Gazelles are very good jumpers, so Linda imagined running and jumping through a field of flowers. As she had fun in her imagination, Linda watched the computer screen. The temperature in her hoof got warmer! When Linda thought about one of her worries, or had other scary thoughts, the hoof got cold. That was because the blood was going from her hoof to her heart to prepare her to run away from danger. When she thought about running, jumping, and having fun, Linda saw that her hoof warmed up again.

Becky suggested to Linda, "You might like to put your anxiety into a container. I am not sure what shape or color the container will be. Perhaps it will be a ball, or maybe a cube, or something else entirely. Notice the color of your container, then attach a faucet to the bottom of it. Turn the faucet, and allow all that anxiety to flow out as the container collapses and the color drains out … Good."

In her imagination, Linda saw the ball that used to hold her anxiety. It looked shrunken and faded, like a balloon when all the air is let out. Linda began to notice how good, how safe, and how calm she felt.

Linda liked biofeedback. Becky was right: biofeedback was like a videogame for the body. Linda learned that she could control what she never knew she could by learning to relax, and by thinking to help herself. It felt wonderful!

# Brownie Bat

Brownie was a brown bat who came to the Ashland Zoo from Vermont. Bats are the only mammals that fly. They are also one of the few mammals that truly hibernate during the Vermont winters. By hibernating they can go all winter without eating. They go into a deep sleep. Their heart rate slows and their body temperature goes down.

The expression "blind as a bat" isn't really accurate. Bats can see, and have a good sense of smell, but instead of using their eyes to fly at night they use a system called echolocation. To do this, Brownie made rapid clicks in his throat. Those clicking sounds bounced off obstacles in his path and their echoes guided him so he could fly without bumping into things in the dark.

Brown bats sleep hanging upside down in dark places during the day. At night they come out and look for insects to eat. Brownie could eat 600 mosquitoes in an hour. His appetite for insects made him very popular at the zoo where nobody liked mosquitoes.

Every morning when the sun came up, Brownie and his cousins returned to their roost to rest. All of the

bats quickly fell asleep except for Brownie, who just couldn't relax enough to even feel sleepy.

One day Brownie confided his problem to his friend, Harry the Hypno-potamus.

Harry said, "I bet Dr. Dan could show you some ways to help yourself with your sleeping problem."

"That would be great," said Brownie. "I'm so tired from not sleeping I don't even feel like eating mosquitoes."

When Harry heard that, he brought Dr. Dan over to see Brownie right away. Dr. Dan watched as Brownie hung upside down from his feet.

"You seem pretty relaxed," the veterinarian said to Brownie. "I'd like to see you tighten the muscles in your right foot."

Brownie squeezed his right foot into a tight little ball.

"Now let the muscles in your foot relax," said Dr. Dan.

Brownie slowly released his tight foot muscles. His right foot did feel more relaxed.

"Now tighten your left foot," said Dr. Dan.

Brownie squeezed his left foot into a tight little ball.

"Now relax your left foot," said Dr. Dan.

Brownie relaxed the muscles in his left foot.

"Next, tighten the muscles in your right leg," said Dr. Dan.

Brownie squeezed his leg muscles as tight as he could.

"Now **relax**," said Dr. Dan. "Notice how all the muscles in that leg feel **loose, limp**, and **relaxed**."

Then Dr. Dan said, "Tighten the muscles in your left leg, hold it, then **relax even more**."

Brownie sighed as he felt the muscles in his left leg get loose, limp, and relaxed.

"That **wave of relaxation**," said Dr. Dan, " is taking you **down** even **deeper relaxed**. Tighten all the muscles in your tummy and back while noticing how **relaxed** your legs and feet are—so **comfortable**, so relaxed, all those muscles loose, limp and **relaxed**. Now your tummy and back are joining the comfort as the **wave of relaxation** continues taking you down **deeper** and **deeper**.

"Tighten one wing, and then **relax** even more all the way to the tips. Now the other wing, tighten and then twice as **relaxed**, going deeper and **deeper**."

Brownie was already beginning to notice his neck, head and face relaxing. Then, as he tightened those muscles and released the tension and tightness, he felt twice as relaxed as he had been before.

Brownie could hear Dr. Dan saying softly, "From the top of your head at the bottom, to the bottom of your feet at the top, relaxed from head to toe. Growing very sleepy. Perhaps you will pretend to pretend that you are sleeping, and then pretend that you are not pretending.

"You might wish to fly high in your imagination up into the clouds—white and fluffy, **drifting** and **floating**. If anything drifts into your thoughts that interfere with sleep, you can turn the stuff into fluff and float it off with the clouds. Stuff becoming fluff and drifting **farther** and **farther** away, so **relaxing**, so **peaceful**."

As Brownie hung upside down in his roost—so familiar, so safe and comfortable—he imagined a gentle breeze rocking him gently to sleep. Soon he was sleeping. *ZZZZzzzz*. Fast asleep.

# Marlene Worry Warthog

Marlene was an African pig. She was not cute, or cuddly, or graceful, but she was amazing. Marlene could live in an area without any water for several months. She liked to take sand baths, and she loved rubbing her bristly body against trees and termite mounds. Marlene was a surprisingly fast runner, even backwards. She couldn't see very well, but if she smelled or heard an enemy, she would bolt backwards into a hole, defending herself with her very long tusks.

Marlene came to live at the Ashland Zoo when she was a baby. She was called a "warthog" because she had four large, lumpy warts on her face. Harry the Hypno-potamus called her "Worry Warthog", because Marlene worried about everything. When she got up in the morning, all of Marlene's worries woke up with her: What if the sun doesn't shine? What if the visitors at the Ashland Zoo think I am ugly? What if Elkins, the elephant, gets sunburned and turns pink? All of this what-ifing made the warthog feel nervous all the time.

Harry noticed that sometimes Marlene was so busy what-ifing and worrying that she forgot to have fun

and be happy. One day, he said to her, "You know, I used to worry about a lot of things."

"What things?" asked Marlene.

"Oh, stuff," said Harry. "I worried about all kinds of stuff. For instance, when I heard that the zoo was going to move me to a new home, I was very nervous."

"You don't look worried now," said the worry warthog.

"That's because I learned to use hypnosis," Harry said.

"Hypnosis? What's that?" asked Marlene.

"It's a way of using your imagination to help yourself," the hypno-potamus replied.

Marlene snorted. "I already use my imagination. I imagine that nobody likes me. I imagine that it might rain on the zoo picnic and ruin everything. I imagine a rock falling on my toe and squashing it …"

Harry said, "Using your imagination is like riding an elevator. It can take you down to a place where you probably don't want to be, a place full of worries and fears, but it can also take you up to incredible heights

and wonderful places. With your imagination, you can take the elevator all the way up to the sky and fly with the eagles."

"You already have a great imagination," said Harry. "You can imagine all this bad stuff, so why not use your imagination to imagine good stuff. You could use your imagination to help yourself with the what-ifing."

The worried warthog thought about what Harry had told her. She said, "You know, Harry, sometimes friends are like elevators: they can support you and lift you up, or they can take you down."

After Harry and Marlene talked some more, the worried warthog decided to use hypnosis and her imagination to help herself. She wanted to ride the elevator up, not down, and be the kind of friend who lifts your spirits up, not one who takes you down.

Marlene was ready to ride the elevator of her imagination up to some place wonderful. As she got onto the elevator, she dragged all her baggage full of worries and what-ifs with her. All that weight made the elevator so heavy it started to go down, not up. Marlene knew she needed to do something. She used her wonderful imagination to imagine a WIFT, a What-if Trash. She imagined the WIFT to be pink,

because pink was her favorite color. She painted it with daisies, because she loved flowers. She made the WIFT out of steel, because she wanted it to be strong and safe. Marlene's WIFT looked a little bit like a mailbox. It had a slot to stick stuff in, but you couldn't get the stuff back out.

Marlene began to put all her what-ifs and worries into the WIFT. After a while, she discovered that, any time she began to have any nervous feelings … ZING! They shot right into the WIFT. This was a truly amazing WIFT that Marlene made, because it never got too full to put things in, yet it never let the stuff back out. It kept everything safe until the time for the what-if had passed, and then … POOF! … it WIFTED, and just magically disappeared. After that, Marlene could remember to forget, or forget to remember, the what-if that she had put in the WIFT. And with the what-ifs in the WIFT till they WIFT and POOFED, Marlene felt free to remember to remember to do fun stuff. She could ride the elevator of her imagination up, up, up, up, and away.

# Shy Sheryll Turtle

Everyone said that Sheryll was too shy. Sheryll was a turtle who lived in a pond at the Ashland Zoo. When she was in the water, Sheryll stuck her head and feet out of the shell that was her home, and swam bravely around the pond. When she climbed out of the pond to sun herself on a log, the turtle's head and legs disappeared inside her shell.

"Maybe everyone will think I'm just a rock, and not notice me," Sheryll said to herself.

If folks knew that Sheryll was a turtle, they would stop and want to talk to her. She never knew what to say to them. Worse yet, they might want to take her picture, or ask her a question.

Sheryll liked Harry the Hypno-potamus. He spent most of the day in the water, too.

"You are missing out on a lot of fun stuff at the zoo because you are always hiding in your shell," Harry told Sheryll. "If you ask Dr. Dan to teach you self-hypnosis, it could help you to come out of your shell, try new things, meet people, and have more fun."

Dr. Dan was the Ashland Zoo veterinarian. "When you are ready, I can help you to use your imagination to help yourself," he told Sheryll.

The turtle spent the next few days inside her shell, watching the other animals in the zoo. They did look like they were having more fun than she was. She wished that she were brave enough to join in.

Finally, Sheryll told Dr. Dan, "I'm ready for you to help me."

"Your imagination is like a magic carpet," Dr. Dan suggested. "It is a very special carpet, with very special magic. It can take you anywhere you want to be, or back to anywhere you have already been. The carpet can zoom in close, so you can examine things carefully, or you can see things from a distance—a **safe** distance.

"Perhaps the magic carpet of your imagination will take you to a place far away that you have never seen, only **imagined**, or perhaps it will take you to a familiar place, so familiar, so **safe**, and so

**comfortable**. It is your imagination and your magic carpet. You can use it to go anywhere you want, or do anything you chose to do, either with somebody special, or all by yourself. You are **protected** by the magic of your special carpet. Whatever works best for you, whatever you would like, or want, to do, you are in the driver's seat; you are **in control**. Just remember to enjoy yourself on the magic carpet of your imagination."

As Sheryll was thinking about what fun it would be to take a ride on the magic carpet of her imagination, Dr. Dan bent over and picked up something from off the ground. It was a rubber band.

"Oh," he said thoughtfully, "I wonder what we can do with this? Not much, unless we stretch it. We could, if we stretched it, hold a bouquet of flowers together, close up a hole in a piece of cloth or plastic, or make a pony tail."

"I know!" said Sheryll. "It is like the rubber band of a slingshot."

"That's right," said Dr. Dan. " A slingshot doesn't work unless it is stretched; then, it can send things soaring."

Sheryll stuck her head out a little bit, and stretched her neck, while she watched Dr. Dan stretch the rubber band and send an acorn flying. Sheryll pretended to fly with the acorn, and then the acorn became the steering wheel of her magic carpet.

"From my magic carpet, in the distance, I can see Max and Mitch Monkey shooting basketballs at the animal show. I can see Wark Cockatoo singing in the bird show, but I need to zoom in a little closer in order to hear him. I'm amazed that Wark can sing in front of all those people."

"Wark used to get nervous, too, before he performed," the veterinarian told Sheryll, "then he learned self-hypnosis to help him control the anxiety he used to have."

Dr. Dan said, "Imagine that you are swimming in the safety of your own pond, with your legs and neck stretched out, feeling safe and powerful. Notice how easily and comfortably you are speaking with all your familiar friends in the pond: Oster Otter and Norma and Phil Beaver. That's right. Now, bring those good, confident feelings back with you to the log."

Dr Dan told Sheryll the story of the butterfly.

"When I was just a boy," he said, "I was walking in a field one autumn, when I saw a chrysalis hanging on a milkweed plant. I knew that a caterpillar had spun this cocoon, and it would soon emerge as a beautiful monarch butterfly."

"As I watched," Dr. Dan continued, "the cocoon began to tremble and wiggle with life … I wanted to help the butterfly by freeing it from the cocoon, so I cut open the chrysalis with my jackknife. The butterfly looked all wadded up. She tried to unfold her wings to fly, but she just fluttered to the ground and lay there, unable to move. Later, I learned that it is necessary for the butterfly to struggle all by herself to get out of the cocoon. By struggling, she builds up the strength in her wings so she can fly and be free."

"In your imagination," Dr. Dan told Sheryll, "all things are possible. A good imagination is more powerful than bad fears, and a lot more fun. I wonder whether it will be this week, or next, that you will realize that coming out of your shell is easier than you ever thought it would be."

Sheryll first imagined just sticking out her feet, then stretching her neck out. She began to smile at the other animals and the visitors at the zoo. After a while, she began to talk to them.

One day, Harry the Hypno-potamus invited Sheryll to play hide and seek. Sheryll poked her head out of

her shell, and then her arms and her legs and her tail. Through the water, around the trees, rocks, and over the grass she crept, looking for her friend. Soon, many of the animals joined in the game. Sheryll, who was an expert at hiding, found Harry first.

The turtle gave a happy cry. "You're it," she said to the hypno-potamus.

The rest of the animals cheered. Harry cheered the loudest of all, because he was so proud of his friend.

Sheryll laughed. Being a turtle, she decided, was a lot more fun than pretending to be a rock.

# *Jordan Jaguar*

Jordan was a jaguar, the biggest cat in South America. Some people thought that he was a leopard because he had spots, but his cousins, the leopards, lived a half a world away in Africa and Asia.

Jordan could do all sorts of magic tricks. He could make a tennis ball appear out of nowhere, and he could even pull a rabbit out of a hat. There was one thing, though, that he would like to make disappear forever: needles. Jordan needed to be immunized so he wouldn't get sick, and that meant getting stuck with a needle. He was scared of needles. He hated them. Jordan couldn't remember the last time he got a shot, but he was sure that it was bad. Why else would he be so frightened? Jordan's fear got bigger and bigger, like a big black balloon. Just thinking about a shot made his head hurt, his tummy do flip-flops, and his heart beat faster.

One day, Jordan told Harry the Hypno-potamus about his fears. Harry nodded his head in sympathy.

"I used to be scared of needles, too," Harry said, "but I learned to use self-hypnosis and the magic of imagination to help me when I got a shot."

"If you will teach me how to do self-hypnosis, so that my shots won't bother me," Jordan replied, "I'll teach you how some of my magic tricks work."

Harry grinned. "You don't have to give me anything in return. I love to do hypnosis—that's why my name is Harry the Hypno-potamus—but I sure would like to know how you do your magic tricks."

Jordan said, "The secret of magic is this: sometimes the magician will have everyone in the audience focus all their attention on something. While they are concentrating on that particular thing—one of the magician's hands, for instance—they don't even notice when the magician does something quickly with his other hand. The magician might also tell the audience to watch his right hand. A couple of seconds later, he does something to distract them, to make them look somewhere else. In that moment that they are distracted, the magician does something tricky, and the audience doesn't even notice. It looks like it happened by magic."

"Why, that's just like hypnosis," Harry said. "Hypnosis is like being your own magician. Hypnosis is the magic. You use your imagination to think about something fun. You pay so much attention to your daydream that, when something else happens, like a little poke from a needle, you don't even notice. Your imagination can play a magic trick on your brain. In your imagination, you can turn the needle poke into a tickle, or you could pretend that the leg where you are getting the poke isn't even attached to you any more. In your imagination, you could find a switch that turns off the pain to that arm."

"Your imagination is filled with magic," Harry continued. "Imagine a big, beautiful helium balloon attached to the tip of your tail. A helium balloon is special. It's so light that if you don't hang onto the string, it will go right up into the sky."

Jordan liked purple, so he imagined that Harry was tying a big purple balloon onto his spotted tail.

Harry said, "When I let go of the string, you may begin to notice a gentle tug on your tail as the balloon starts to go up higher and higher, your tail feeling light, rising a little at first, and then **more** and **more** as the balloon floats higher and farther. That's right, lifting gently. As I cut the imaginary string, your tail will drift slowly back **down** as you go **deeper** and **deeper relaxed**. That's right, very **deeply** relaxed. When your tail touches the ground, your eyes will close, and you will be as **deeply relaxed** as you need to be. Very good. Yes. **Deeply** relaxed. **Comfortable** and **relaxed**.

"With your eyelids heavy, your eyes closed, I'm going to have you put your paw into my jar of magical rocks. Without looking with your eyes, but rather seeing in your imagination, choose a rock and hold it in your paw. That's right. In your imagination, notice what color the rock is, what color it feels like. See and feel its shape and texture, perhaps what it smells like. Imagine what the rock would taste like if you licked it. Remember, it is your imagination and your magic rock, so it can be anything you want it to be. As you become more curious about the rock, you will begin to notice that the magic from the rock will begin to move, to travel from your paw up toward your shoulder. I'm not sure if that will feel like a tingle, or maybe just a flutter, as that magic begins to move. I wonder, as it reaches your shoulder, which way it will begin to move next as the special magic of imagination fills your body. That's right. Very good.

"I wonder how wonderful it will be for you to bring all that magic from all parts of your body—your fingers, your toes, from the tops of your ears to the tip of your tail—and bring it all together, to come together to a spot on your leg where nothing needs to bother or disturb you, a magic spot so that the poke will be easy and quick, and won't even need to bother you. Then, you can remember to remember to be very proud that you were the boss of your brain and the magician of the magic of your imagination.

"That big black balloon of fear you used to have, it would be all right to pop it, or perhaps you will just untie the knot and let it fly and zoom around the room until it drops to the floor empty, and the fear it used to have is gone. Then it would be all right to stomp on it, or dig a hole and bury it, or put it in the garbage. Your inside brain will find a very good way to get rid of that old fear. Then, breathe in that special kind of pride. Breathe in **self-confidence** and breathe out self-doubt. Breathe in **self-esteem** and breathe out uncertainty."

Harry said, " I like to blow bubbles in my mud puddle when I'm getting shots."

Jordan replied, "I don't really like mud puddles."

"Well," said Harry, "you could blow away any discomfort using a pinwheel or a bubble wand instead."

When Dr. Dan arrived to give Jordan his shot, the jaguar was ready. In his imagination, he made a magic spot on his leg where the shot would go. The magic spot would change any poke into just a tiny tingle that wouldn't need to bother him. Jordan also decided that, since his big black balloon of fear was gone, instead of blowing on a pinwheel, he would fill a purple balloon with pride. So as Dr. Dan gave the jaguar his shot, Jordan blew up a big purple balloon. It was very big, because he had a lot of pride to fill it with. Then he looked down at the magic rock in his paw and realized that the magic wasn't in the rock, it was inside him. It was the magic of his imagination.

# *Oster Otter*

Everyone who came to the Ashland Zoo loved to watch Oster Otter because he always looked like he was having so much fun. Oster loved to make slides in the mud at the edge of the pond, and then zip down the slippery slide with a big splash. As soon as he got into the water, Oster would dive down deep to the bottom of the pond, flip over on his back, float to the surface of the water, and then do it all over again.

Although Oster loved everything about the pond, there was one thing that made him dive down to the bottom and hide under a log. That was thunderstorms. When the skies got dark and storm clouds moved in, Oster grew very nervous. His tummy shivered like jello, his arms and legs got shaky, and he didn't feel good at all. Oster hated thunderstorms.

Haley was a friend of Harry the Hypno-potamus. She came to the zoo almost every day. She loved to watch Oster coast down his mud slide into the pond. Watching him reminded her of riding the roller coaster at the amusement park.

One day, Haley told Oster, "They're making a new roller coaster for the park. Last week, the people who are building it came to my school and asked us to help. They wanted to know what we would like best in a roller coaster. Wade said he would like the ride to be dark. George said that flashing bolts of light would be great. Tricia suggested howling winds. Everybody thought that a spray of water would be cool, too."

The next time Haley saw Oster, she told him, "They finished making the roller coaster, and they used all of our suggestions. Now they are having a contest to name the ride. The winner and a friend get to be the first ones to go on the roller coaster. That's the prize. I've tried to think of a name, but I I'm not good at that. I sure would love to win, though."

"How about 'STORM'?" asked Oster.

"That's a great name for the new roller coaster," Haley said.

The park thought so, too, and awarded Oster the prize.

Oster was very excited. He had never won anything before.

"You've got to come with me on my prize-winning first ride on 'STORM,'" he told Haley.

Haley was thrilled.

"I've never been on a roller coaster before," Oster said.

"You'll love it," Haley said. "It's like coasting down your slide into the pond, only way better!"

Still, Oster felt a little nervous.

Haley said, "I know a way for you to use your imagination to help yourself get over your nervousness. It's called 'hypnosis.' I learned it from my friend, Harry the Hypno-potamus."

"Harry talks about hypnosis sometimes," Oster said. "He says it is lots of fun. Could we try some hypnosis right now?"

"Sure," said Haley. "In your imagination, go to your favorite ocean beach. Breathe in the peacefulness of that special place. Listen for the sound of the waves, the endless song of the sea. Each wave is bringing in **comfort** and taking away stress, bringing in **relaxation** and taking away tension. Notice the sun sparkling like diamonds on the water. Perhaps you can feel the warmth of the sun on your back, or a cool, calm breeze caressing your face. It's **so relaxing**, so **peaceful**."

Haley continued, "Imagine taking whatever nervousness or fears that you have, and putting them in the sand of the beach, building up the pile as big as it needs to be to hold whatever worries you need to put there. I'm not sure if it will look like a sand castle, or just a big pile of sand. When you are sure that most, or all, of the worries and concerns that you need to put there are buried in the sand, let your head nod to signal me."

"Now," said Haley, "you will notice something very interesting. The tide is beginning to turn; the tide is coming in. Each wave is getting closer and closer to your pile of worries buried in the sand. First, the waves are just nipping at the bottom, and then more and more, each wave bringing in **comfort** and taking away stress, bringing in **relaxation** and taking away tension, each wave bringing in **comfort**, **courage**, and **confidence**, while taking away the stress buried in the pile of sand. In with **calm**, out with worries, until the sand is completely smooth. That's right. Excellent!"

Haley continued, "Notice how different you feel, perhaps lighter. Perhaps you will feel like something very heavy that you were carrying on your back is now gone."

Oster was ready to ride. He was very excited, yet he felt very calm. Haley and Oster decided to sit in the very front seat. The roller coaster started up a steep hill and plunged down into darkness, then there were bright lights, loud cracking noises and howling winds. The coaster went up, down, and around. At the very end, a spray of water got them both right in the face. It was so much fun! They couldn't wait to do it again.

Haley told Oster, "Your prize-winning name, 'STORM,' is perfect, because that roller coaster is a lot like a storm."

"I'm surprised," said Oster, "because I thought I hated storms, but I loved this ride."

The next time the sky got dark, gray and stormy, Oster noticed that he didn't need to hide at the bottom of the pond under a log. One evening, after a very hot day, he saw heat lightening in the distance. It reminded him of fireworks on the Fourth of July, and he felt calm and okay. A few days later, a big storm was predicted. Oster thought about "STORM," the roller-coaster ride, and how much fun it was. Thinking about winning the contest and taking the first ride, and remembering everything that made it so special, made Oster feel good, comfortable, calm, and relaxed. The storm blew in with winds, rain, thunder and lightening. Oster discovered that he liked the sound the raindrops made on the pond, and the way the lightening lit up the sky. He had never known that he liked them, because he had always hidden under the log. Now, he discovered that he liked storms a little, and he loved "STORM" a lot.

# Dabney Gorilla

Dabney was the biggest and strongest male gorilla at the Ashland Zoo. In the world of gorillas, which are the largest of all the apes, his strength and size made Dabney the boss, or leader.

Dabney didn't feel like a leader. He had a secret that he didn't want any of the other gorillas to know: he was afraid of small, dark places. At night, when all the gorillas went into a covered enclosure to sleep, Dabney slept outside where he could see the streetlight. The comforting glow from the light made him feel safe, and he was able to get to sleep.

When the other gorillas asked Dabney why he didn't sleep inside with them, Dabney answered, "I have to stay outside. That way, if anything dangerous happens, I can protect you."

This is what Dabney told his friends, but the truth was, he was too scared to go inside. The big gorilla tried to get over his fears, but they only got worse and worse. Finally, he went to see Dr. Dan, the zoo veterinarian.

"I feel so silly," Dabney whispered. "I'm a gorilla. I'm supposed to be brave and strong. Sometimes, I do feel brave, but when I have to go inside a little dark place, I get as scared as a little baby."

Dabney screwed his lips into an embarrassed little grin. "I was going to say, 'scared as a mouse,'" he chuckled, "but those little guys aren't afraid of the dark. They **love** little dark places."

Dr. Dan looked up at the big gorilla standing beside his desk. "I can teach you how to help yourself with hypnosis," he said. "Look out my window, and I'll show you how it works."

Dabney didn't see how looking out a window could help him get over his fear, but he loped across the room, swaying his long, furry arms. The gorillas lived in a large enclosure on the side of a mountain. Dabney could see it all from Dr. Dan's office window.

"Imagine that you are on the top of the mountain," Dr. Dan suggested. "It can be any season that you want

it to be: summer, winter, fall, or spring. From the mountain, you can see everything very clearly."

"There are different ways that you could chose to come down the mountain," Dr. Dan continued. "If it is winter, there is a sled, a snowmobile, a pair of skis and a snowboard. In warmer weather there will be a bicycle, a scooter, a skateboard and roller blades. Perhaps there will also be something else, hidden behind a tree. You are the boss of your imagination, so you can decide to come down the mountain any way you choose. Perhaps you will just want to walk down along the beautiful path."

"It is summer on the top of my mountain," Dabney said. "I can see vines, lots of vines. I'm going to swing from vine to vine with my big, strong arms. That's my favorite way to come down the mountain."

Dr. Dan said, "Notice the smell of the forest: so familiar, **so safe**. Breathe in that smell as you go **down** deeper and **deeper**. Notice the shades of color, and the sun sparkling through the trees. Listen for the sounds of the branches rustling as you swing **down** the mountain, going **down deeper**, swinging, each swing taking you **deeper** and deeper **down**. Feel the vine grasped in your hand. Notice your strength outside, and going inside, **stronger, deeper**. The trees are

getting closer together. There is less sunlight coming through. The spaces between the trees are smaller. They feel cozy and safe. You feel **calm, comfortable, confident**, and **in control** as you continue **down** the mountain. When you reach the bottom, you will be as relaxed as you need to be. Let your head nod to signal me when you have reached the bottom and feel comfortably relaxed. Excellent. Very good.

"It is interesting that your inside, relaxing brain can speak to me even without talking. There is a finger on one of your hands that is the 'yes' finger. I don't know which finger is the 'yes' one, but your inside brain knows. If I ask you a question and the answer is 'yes,' that finger—the 'yes' finger—will start to move all by itself. The 'yes' finger will move just a little at first, feeling lighter, and then move up to tell me that the answer to the question is 'yes.' It will be fun to discover which finger is the 'yes' finger. Remember: don't try to move any of your fingers. Just relax, and let your inside brain show you which is the 'yes' finger today."

Dr. Dan asked Dabney, "Do you have black fur?"

Dabney's right index finger began to move, at first just slightly, like a twitch, and then a little more.

57

"Good," said Dr. Dan. "Your right-pointing finger is the 'yes' one. Now, won't it be interesting to discover which is the 'no' finger? When I ask you a question, and the answer is 'no,' that finger will move."

Dr. Dan asked, "Are you the same size as a rabbit?"

Dabney's left thumb began to move.

"Oh!" said Dr. Dan. "I see that your left thumb is the 'no' finger. Very good! Since you never have to answer a question in hypnosis unless you want to, there is another finger. It's called the 'I'm-not-ready-to-answer-that-question-yet' finger. Allow your inner mind, your inside brain, to show you which finger that is."

The little finger on Dabney's left hand began to move.

"Good," said Dr. Dan. "Your right-pointing finger is your 'yes' finger, and your left thumb is your 'no' finger. Your 'I'm-not-ready-to-answer-that-question-yet' finger is the little finger on your left hand."

"Now", said Dr. Dan, "imagine that it is late in the day. The sun is setting. In the west, the sky is a brilliant orange. Tomorrow, it's going to be a beautiful day. In your imagination, move closer to your enclosure on the mountainside. Notice how comfortably relaxed you are as the sun is setting deeper and deeper, so

peaceful. Let your 'yes' finger signal to me when you are comfortable and relaxed."

Dabney's right index finger drifted upward.

"Good", said Dr. Dan. "Now, imagine that you are standing in the doorway of the enclosure, with your face turned toward the welcoming darkness. Behind you, the sun is setting. Notice how calm, comfortable, confident, and in control you feel. That's right. It would be all right to take a step further in as you take a deep breath of self-confidence. Yes, breathe in self-confidence, and breathe out self-doubt. Very good. When you are calm, comfortable and relaxed, let that 'yes' finger signal to me. Dark and safe: very good. Deeper inside. As you turn around, feeling calm, confident and very safe, the sun has set. Darkness is drifting in, comfortably, easily. Let one of your fingers signal me that you are doing just fine."

Dabney began to become a little anxious, and his right thumb began to move.

"Ah," said Dr. Dan, "I see that your 'no' finger has answered me. Just focus your attention on your breathing. Breathe way down **deep** in your belly. Breathing in **comfort**, and breathing out stress. That's right, slow and **deep**. Isn't it interesting that each time

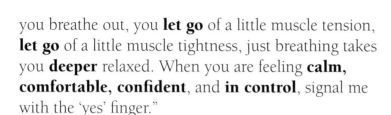

you breathe out, you **let go** of a little muscle tension, **let go** of a little muscle tightness, just breathing takes you **deeper** relaxed. When you are feeling **calm, comfortable, confident**, and **in control**, signal me with the 'yes' finger."

Dabney's pointer finger, the "yes" finger, began to move.

"Good. Very good. I wonder how wonderful it will be for you to lie down, stretch out, and get even more comfortable. You may notice that your eyelids are becoming very heavy, **heavy and relaxed**, drifting **down**, closing, safely, darkly, as you go deeper and deeper relaxed. That's right, stretch out as you get even more comfortable, **even more** relaxed. It would be all right to fall asleep in that **safe**, dark, enclosed space.

"Since, in your imagination, you can do anything, you can make your imagination go fast-forward to sunrise. The first rays of the morning sun are shining into your enclosure. Notice how good you feel, how proud you are. When you are feeling happy and proud about what you were able to accomplish, let your 'yes' finger signal me. That's great!

"The days ahead are going to be especially exciting. I don't know when, whether it will be this week or

next, that you will look back and realize that you have achieved your goal by moving forward in the direction you wished to go. You are going in the direction of success, leaving your old fear behind. Know that you were able to do it entirely on your own, using all your self-confidence and courage, and your own control."

That night, Dabney slept with the other gorillas in the dark enclosure. In the morning, he stretched his powerful body, and beat on his chest in triumph. Controlling the fear that once controlled him felt wonderful. Dabney really did feel big and strong, and for the first time, he knew that he was a leader. He knew that he was the boss of all the gorillas, but most of all, Dabney was the boss of himself.

# Elkins Elephant

Elkins was an African elephant who lived at the Ashland Zoo. Unlike his Asian cousins, Elkins had very big ears. They were shaped like the map of Africa. Everything about Elkins was big. When he was full-grown, he could weigh as much as four tons.

Elkins's trunk was very special. He used it to pick up food, drink water, and breathe. He could suck up water with his trunk, and then squirt it into his mouth. His favorite thing was to take a dirt bath. Elkins would pick up the dirt with his trunk, then blow it all over his back. With his very clever trunk, Elkins could break off a branch of a tree, or pick up something as small as a peanut.

Elkins had six sets of teeth, called "molars," on the top, and six sets of molars on the bottom. When one set of Elkins's molars was worn down by chewing on tough branches, another set of teeth moved forward, pushing out the old, worn-down ones. When elephants have used up all six sets of teeth, they will no longer be able to eat and grind up food, and they will die.

Elkins knew how important it was to take good care

of his teeth, but he hated going to the dentist. He got so nervous that he shook all over, and couldn't hold still so the dentist could work on his teeth. Finally, he went to see Dr. Kay, the zoo's dentist. Dr. Kay was very nice and very gentle. She told Elkins a story about her friend, John, who liked to row out into the middle of the lake.

"It was so peaceful there," said Dr. Kay. "John could feel the gentle rocking of the boat, making him feel even more **comfortable** and **relaxed**."

"I heard a story about a movie that was being made on a lake in Mt. Dora, Florida," Elkins said. "They painted everything in the town pink for the movie, and they taught an elephant how to water ski. I'm not sure that I would like to water ski, but I think I would like being out in a boat. I can imagine what it would be like, floating and rocking in a boat. It makes me feel good, like when my mother used to rock me with her trunk when I was little."

Elkins got nice and comfortable as Dr. Kay continued her story about her friend, John.

"John liked to imagine the world of the fish, and what it was like to live underwater, and all the things he could see there. He was having fun imagining, when something bumped into his boat. He could see that it was a very big fish. The fish was tangled in fish line, and a fishhook was caught in his mouth. John reached over to catch the fish so that he could help him. He tried to get the fishhook out of the fish's mouth, but the fish was wiggling and squirming too much.

"John was having a very difficult time. All he wanted to do was to help the fish. Suddenly, the fish looked up into John's eyes, and saw the kindness there, and became very **still** and **calm**. That's right, **very still** and **calm**. John was able to **easily** take the hook out of the fish's mouth, and gently put the fish back into the water. As the fish swam away, he waved his tail to say 'thank-you.' John smiled and returned to the underwater world of his imagination."

Elkins smiled. "I like that story," he said.

Elkins also liked Dr. Kay. While Dr. Kay cleaned and polished Elkins's teeth, the elephant opened his mouth very wide. Elkins imagined that he was holding a fishing pole with his trunk, in a boat on the lake, as the boat rocked gently back and forth. Then, he imagined following a fish underwater. Using his trunk

as a snorkel, Elkins could stay underwater for a very long time. He didn't even hear Dr. Kay say that she was all done. He was having too much fun fishing in his imagination.

63

# Valerie Walrus

Valerie Walrus lived in a large pool at the Ashland Zoo with her cousins, the seals and the sea lions. Like them, Valerie was a pinniped. Instead of legs, these sea animals have flippers to help them walk on land. Most of the time, though, Valerie and her cousins stayed in the water. She used her flippers to steer when she was swimming.

Valerie liked cold weather and ice covered with snow. She had two big tusks, which she used to help pull her big body out of the water and onto the rocky shores. Her bristly whiskers were very sensitive, and sent important information about her surroundings to her brain.

Valerie's thick, wrinkled skin was a cinnamon brown color. However, when the water was very cold, she would appear to be almost white. In warmer weather, Valerie turned pink. She had a special friend named Tom. He was bigger than Valerie. Tom weighed 1,500 pounds.

One day, when Valerie and Tom were swimming, one of Valerie's flippers started to hurt. The pain lasted

for weeks and weeks. After a while, Valerie's flipper just wouldn't work right. She had trouble walking on the shore around her pool. She even had trouble swimming. Finally, the zookeepers took Valerie to see Dr. Dan, the zoo veterinarian.

Dr. Dan wasn't sure what was wrong. He told Valerie that she needed an MRI.

"An MRI," Dr. Dr. Dan explained, "is a special picture that shows things on our insides even better than an X-ray. For us to take that MRI picture, you need to lie down on a special table. After you get settled, the table moves into a tube. It is important to lie very still. When the table is all the way inside the tube, the machine will start to make a very loud noise. The noise sounds a little like a jackhammer. A jackhammer is the machine that workers sometimes use to help break up the cement when they are fixing the roads or a sidewalk."

Valerie felt a little scared. She talked about her fears with her friend, Harry the Hypno-potamus. Harry had an idea. He whispered in the walrus's ear, "Hypnosis can help. If you use self-hypnosis, the MRI won't need to bother you. In fact, it will be fun."

Harry had already taught Valerie how to use self-hypnosis when Dr. Dan had to give her a shot, so she decided to use her imagination and pretend that she was going to be the first walrus in space. The MRI machine was her rocket ship.

Using her tusks and the flipper that worked okay, Valerie climbed up on the table and prepared to blast off. As the table moved her into the tube, Valerie imagined being in her spaceship with her seatbelt securely fastened, feeling very safe and secure, holding very still as she waited to rocket into space.

The engines were ready for lift-off. All systems go. Everything safe and ready for take-off. Ten … nine … eight … more relaxed with each number. Seven … six … five … four … very relaxed. Three … two … one … Blast-off!

Valerie imagined that she could see the earth getting smaller and smaller. She was excited, yet relaxed and comfortable, her body adjusting to outer space. She could hear the roar of the powerful engines as she passed through a meteor shower, then the rocket engines got quiet as Valerie circled a planet. The

powerful engines revved up again as she took off for another planet. Every time the rocket engines got quiet, another planet came into view. Each planet was more beautiful and amazing than the last.

Sometimes, Valerie imagined walking around on the surface of the planet. She also liked to pretend she was weightless, floating in space. After a while, Valerie went off again, flying comfortably through space, safe and secure inside her spaceship. It was an awesome trip.

When the MRI study was completed, Valerie's rocket ship brought her back to earth, calm and relaxed. As the MRI table slid Valerie out, she couldn't wait to tell her friend, Tom Walrus, about her wonderful adventure.

# Wark Cockatoo

One sunny morning in July, a huge crowd gathered at the Ashland Zoo. There were fathers and mothers, uncles and aunts, grandmas and grandpas, and lots and lots of children. All of them were headed for The Bird Show to see Wark, their favorite performer.

Wark was a cockatoo, a bird who belongs to the parrot family. He had lovely white feathers and a glorious golden crown. In Australia, where Wark lived before he went to the zoo, the farmers thought the cockatoo was a pest. He could be very noisy, and he liked to eat the farmers' seeds, nuts, berries and fruit.

At the Ashland Zoo, though, Wark was a star. The cockatoo had learned to ride a bicycle. When he pedaled into The Bird Show on his little bike, all the children cheered and clapped their hands. After he rode around for a while, Wark would hop off his bicycle and over to the trapeze. Holding the bar tightly with his feet, he would swing back and forth, higher and higher. When the swinging stopped, Wark would do flips around the trapeze bar.

After a while, the children would yell to him, "Sing, Wark, sing!" This was the part of the show they liked the best.

"My bonnie lies over the ocean, my bonnie lies over the sea," the little cockatoo would sing.

Singing, though, made Wark feel very nervous. "My voice sounds scratchy," he would say to himself. "My singing doesn't sound pretty, like a canary's or a robin's."

The cockatoo began to worry. As the days went by, Wark worried more and more, and it got harder and harder for him to sing. Sometimes he had trouble concentrating. He would forget some of the words to his songs. Finally, on that sunny morning in July, when the children called out, "Sing, Wark, sing," the little cockatoo stood frozen like an ice cube. When he opened his beak to sing, instead of the loud, clear, wonderful song the children loved, a tiny squeak came out. The sound was not a song, just a hoarse little, scratchy little squeal. Wark had forgotten every single word to his song.

The children clapped to encourage him, but Wark was mortified. He hopped down from his trapeze bar and got on his little bicycle. Wark's feathers drooped. He hung his head. His bicycle wobbled. Still, the children clapped and clapped. They loved the little cockatoo.

For the next few days, Wark refused to leave his roost. The zookeeper in charge of birds got worried. She called Dr. Dan, the Ashland Zoo veterinarian.

"Wark just sits on his roost all day with his head tucked under his wing," the zookeeper said. "He isn't singing, and he doesn't ride his bicycle."

When Dr. Dan arrived, he looked Wark over very carefully. Wark's feathery body seemed all right, but Wark looked sad. When Dr. Dan asked him why, Wark answered in a scratchy voice, "I can't sing anymore."

Dr. Dan nodded sympathetically. "I think," he said, "that you worried so much you got all tightened up. When that happens, your throat can get so tight and small that no sound comes out. You can forget things, important things, like the words to songs. Would you like me to show you a way to help yourself?"

Wark drew his head from under his wing and straightened up.

"I'll teach you about belly breathing," said Dr. Dan. "It's a great way to get rid of some of that tightness and loosen up."

Wark gave a happy little "peep." "That sounds good," he said.

"Take a slow, deep breath," said Dr. Dan. "Pull that breath right into your belly. With every breath, fill your belly up with air. Feel your belly, instead of your chest, rise and fall with every breath. Slow and **deep**, rising and falling, notice how just breathing makes you feel **more** and more **relaxed**."

As Wark took in deep breaths and let them out, watching his tummy rise and fall, he felt his muscles loosen.

"Now," said Dr. Dan, "find a spot to focus on while you take a deep breath in."

While the cockatoo swung back and forth on his perch, breathing with his belly in and out, he saw a round, rusty spot on the wall of his cage. He focused on that. As Wark continued to stare at the spot, focusing all his attention on the spot, he let his breath out, noticing how relaxed his chest felt.

69

"When you take your next deep breath," said Dr. Dan, "keep focusing on your spot. At the same time, push down gently with your feet on the perch as you tighten all the muscles below your belly."

Wark tightened the muscles in his feet and legs all the way up to his belly. When he did that, he noticed that it made his body seem taller.

"Focus even more on your spot as you exhale and relax all your muscles," said Dr. Dan. "When you take your next breath in, observe your spot even more closely, tensing your whole body."

As Wark exhaled, he relaxed his whole body. He noticed that his mind was sharp, focused, and alert, yet his whole body felt comfortable and relaxed. The cockatoo kept on practicing. Each time he did this, it became easier and easier to stay focused, yet relaxed. Wark remembered the good times he had spent performing and singing, and he felt all that happiness once again.

Dr. Dan said, "You thought you couldn't **do this**, of course, perhaps you shouldn't even **do it**, but now you may realize it is something **you can do now**."

"Next," said Dr. Dan, "you might want to see, feel, and hear the whole performance in your imagination, just as you want it to be. Pretend that you are watching it on a big screen DVD. **You control** the remote. You can speed the performance up or slow it down. You can rewind it and fix it until it is just the way you want it to be."

"You know," said Wark, "I sing beautifully when I'm only practicing. It's when I'm in front of the audience that I get so nervous."

"That happens to a lot of people," Dr. Dan said. "Why don't you just think 'practice' when you perform."

"Remember a time when you felt particularly confident," said Dr. Dan. "In your imagination, float back through time and space until you are actually there. Now, feel all over again how really proud and sure of yourself you are. Let yourself feel again and again that 'can do' attitude. Let that strength and that pride flow through you. As you tighten and clench your right foot on your perch, feel that confidence and pride grow even stronger, the tighter you clench. Remember a few other times when you felt particularly sure of yourself."

As Wark felt that sureness all over again, he once more clenched his right foot.

Dr. Dan suggested, "It will be interesting to note that, in the future, any time you clench your right foot, you will feel that sense of **pride**, and that 'can do' sureness increase."

Dr. Dan said, "Go back in your imagination to another time when you were feeling nervous and worried. As you remember that time and those negative feelings, let them flow down your left leg into your left foot, and let them collect there. When you are pretty sure most of those bad feelings are collected there, you can open your clenched left foot, wiggle your toes, and let go of those nervous feelings."

Dr. Dan waited while the little cockatoo followed his suggestions. Then he said, "As you begin to clench your right foot, feel all that **confidence** and **pride** flow through you."

As Wark clenched his right foot, feeling confidence and pride flow through him, Dr. Dan told him, "I call this 'The Stein Clenched Fist Technique.'"

"I call it wonderful!" said Wark.

# Max and Mitch Monkey

Max and Mitch were Black Howler Monkeys. They came to the Ashland zoo from the tropical forests of Central America. Howler monkeys are very good at howling. That's how they got their name. Like roosters who "cock-a-doodle-do" as the sun rises, howler monkeys howl to announce the dawning of a new day. Forest friends can hear their howling from two miles away.

The zookeepers at Ashland Zoo discovered that Mitch was very good at throwing things. Every time they gave the monkeys fruit, Mitch would eat the banana, but any round fruit, such as an orange or an apple, he used as a basketball. He would throw the fruit into a wastebasket about 20 feet away. He made a perfect basket almost all the time.

When Mitch threw his fruit into the basket, Max watched to see how he did it. After awhile, Max, too, started throwing and making baskets. Like Mitch, Max was a very good shot.

The zookeepers asked Mitch and Max if they would like to be in the animal show at the zoo. Garver, who was one of the animal trainers, taught Mitch and Max how to throw a basketball into a basketball hoop. Mitch and Max liked to play against each other and see who could make the most baskets. Each monkey wanted to be the best; each wanted to win.

Mitch was very serious about competing. Sometimes, he got so nervous before a game that he got a tummy ache. If he didn't win, Mitch felt like a loser. He punched the basketball, said bad things to Max, and HOWLED!!!

One day, when Mitch was punching and howling, Garver, the trainer, said, "You know, Mitch, there is a way that you can feel like a winner even when you lose. Winning is not under your control. The only thing you can control is how well you throw the ball. How well or how badly any other monkey does is not under your control."

Garver said, "There are a lot of other things that you have no control over. For instance, if the audience cheers louder for Max than they do for you, or if you don't get to shoot baskets first, or if your daddy

doesn't make it to the game in time to watch you perform—you can't change those things. I call them the 'U.C.s.' That stands for 'uncontrollables'. They are the things that you can't control. They just get in the way. If you let them, they keep you from concentrating on the ball and shooting baskets. These thoughts and worries can keep you from doing your best. You need to get rid of them."

Mitch used his imagination to think about all the ways he could let go of the U.C.s. He could attach them to a kite, and when the kite got really high, he could let go of the string. He could also bury them in the ground, or lock the U.C.s up in a safe. Sometimes, he liked to put them in a trash compactor, or watch them go down the drain.

Garver showed Mitch a way he could program in success and program out mistakes.

"Think of a positive sign, such as a thumbs up," said Garver. "Every time you throw a ball and it goes into the basket just the way you want, give yourself the thumbs up, and say, "Yes!"

That is exactly what Mitch did: he gave himself the thumbs up every time he made a basket, programming it into his brain. When Mitch shot and missed the basket, he gave himself a different signal to get rid of his mistake. He let it go and programmed it out.

First, Mitch practiced in his imagination. He imagined making baskets and programming it into his brain; he imagined giving himself the program-out signal when he imagined missing a basket. He always ended his imaginings, or what Garver called his "self-hypnosis," by making baskets and having a feeling of confidence and a "can do" attitude. As Mitch took a big breath in, he filled his lungs and his whole body with an "I can do it" kind of feeling. As he let the breath out, he got rid of his fears and any bad thoughts. In practice and in competition, Mitch continued to give himself those powerful signals, programming his brain and body for success.

Mitch listened as Garver said, "Whether you think you can, or you think you can't, you are right. Thinking positive, good thoughts helps athletes do their best. If athletes are thinking that they probably won't do very well, they are right: they won't do well. Thinking good thoughts, and saying to yourself, "I can do this; I have practiced hard and I am ready," will help you to do your best. No one can be perfect all the time. Striving to do things perfectly causes frustration and anxiety,

but working toward doing your very best is a great goal. Having fun doing it is also very important."

"Thanks, Garver, for helping me to help myself," Mitch said.

The monkey practiced the things he had learned, and he discovered that he enjoyed shooting baskets with Max a whole lot more. He could feel like a winner because doing his best was under his control. Now he only howled at dawn.

# Cory and Candy Chimpanzee

Cory and his cousin Candy were chimpanzees who lived at the Ashland Zoo. Their relatives came from the rain forests, the woodlands, and the grasslands of Africa. When fully grown, the chimps would be four to five feet tall—almost as big as an adult human. Their favorite foods were fruits, honey, leaves, flowers, ants, and termites.

When Cory was just a baby, he began to suck his right thumb. It made him feel good as he clung to his mother's back while she jumped from tree to tree. Cory became very good at sucking his thumb. He sucked it almost all the time without even thinking about it. He could even do it in his sleep.

Like most chimpanzees, Cory was very smart. He even learned to use a stick to dig up a meal of yummy ants. Cory would happily feast on insects every single day, but he had a problem: he needed two hands to use the stick, and one hand was always in his mouth sucking his thumb! Cory loved to suck his thumb, but he also loved those ants and termites. He didn't know what to do, so he went to ask his cousin, Candy.

Candy listened sympathetically to Cory's tale. As she listened, she nibbled nervously on her fingernails. Even after Cory finished speaking and sat sucking his thumb, waiting for her answer, Candy continued to bite her nails.

Just then, Harry the Hypno-potamus came waddling along on his way home from a mud bath. Cory told Harry about his problem.

"I want to quit," Cory said, "but I don't know how. I don't even know if I can. I've always sucked my thumb."

"You could help yourself with hypnosis," said Harry.

"Hypnosis? What's that?" asked Cory.

"It's a way of using your mind to help yourself," Harry replied. "By thinking certain thoughts on purpose, you can control what you never knew you could." Harry gave his friend a great big hippo grin. "Let's go see Dr. Dan. He's the zoo veterinarian. He can show you how."

Cory and Harry hurried to Dr. Dan's office. Candy had to help her mother, so she went home, biting her nails all the way.

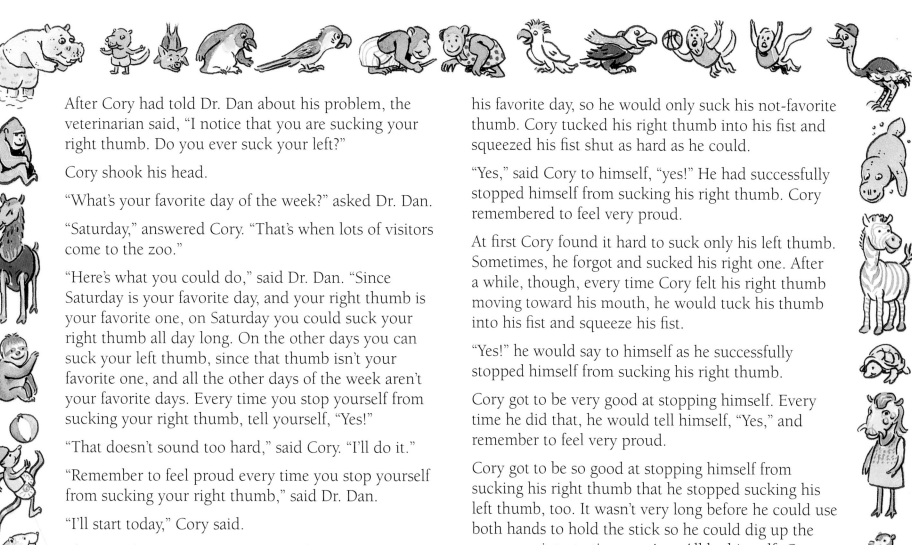

After Cory had told Dr. Dan about his problem, the veterinarian said, "I notice that you are sucking your right thumb. Do you ever suck your left?"

Cory shook his head.

"What's your favorite day of the week?" asked Dr. Dan.

"Saturday," answered Cory. "That's when lots of visitors come to the zoo."

"Here's what you could do," said Dr. Dan. "Since Saturday is your favorite day, and your right thumb is your favorite one, on Saturday you could suck your right thumb all day long. On the other days you can suck your left thumb, since that thumb isn't your favorite one, and all the other days of the week aren't your favorite days. Every time you stop yourself from sucking your right thumb, tell yourself, "Yes!"

"That doesn't sound too hard," said Cory. "I'll do it."

"Remember to feel proud every time you stop yourself from sucking your right thumb," said Dr. Dan.

"I'll start today," Cory said.

The next day was easy. It was Saturday, so Cory would do what he usually did. On Sunday, as soon as Cory woke up, he started to put his right thumb in his mouth. Suddenly he remembered that Sunday was not his favorite day, so he would only suck his not-favorite thumb. Cory tucked his right thumb into his fist and squeezed his fist shut as hard as he could.

"Yes," said Cory to himself, "yes!" He had successfully stopped himself from sucking his right thumb. Cory remembered to feel very proud.

At first Cory found it hard to suck only his left thumb. Sometimes, he forgot and sucked his right one. After a while, though, every time Cory felt his right thumb moving toward his mouth, he would tuck his thumb into his fist and squeeze his fist.

"Yes!" he would say to himself as he successfully stopped himself from sucking his right thumb.

Cory got to be very good at stopping himself. Every time he did that, he would tell himself, "Yes," and remember to feel very proud.

Cory got to be so good at stopping himself from sucking his right thumb that he stopped sucking his left thumb, too. It wasn't very long before he could use both hands to hold the stick so he could dig up the yummy, minty-tasting termites. All by himself, Cory had stopped sucking his thumb—because he could.

Cory was so excited about controlling what he never knew he could, that he went to tell his cousin, Candy.

"That's great," said Candy. "I wish I could control my nail-biting like that. Sometimes my fingers get really sore."

Chimpanzees spend about an hour every day grooming each other. They sit together in a friendly group picking burs, insects, and dirt out of each other's hair. It was difficult for Candy, who had chewed away all her fingernails, to groom the other chimps.

"I wish I had long, beautiful nails like the other chimps," Candy said, "but I don't know how to stop biting my nails."

"It's a habit," said Cory, "just like my thumb-sucking. It's something you do really well. You don't even have to think about it."

"Do you think I could ever stop?" asked Candy.

"We could ask Dr. Dan," said Cory. "Let's go see him."

On their way to the zoo veterinarian's office, Cory told Candy about all the things he had learned about thinking on purpose and controlling what he never knew he could.

After Candy told Dr. Dan about her nail biting, the veterinarian took several bottles of nail polish from his desk drawer.

"Pick out your favorite color," he said.

Candy picked red. Dr. Dan painted two nails on Candy's left hand and three nails on her right hand red.

"You can bite the unpainted nails just as much as you want or need to," Dr. Dan suggested. "You might be interested to discover that you can leave the painted nails alone."

Every night before she went to bed, Candy would imagine how lovely her nails were going to look. Each time she stopped herself from biting the painted nails, she felt so proud that she gave herself a little pat on the back. If Candy felt one hand starting to move up towards her mouth, her other hand—her helper hand—would reach out to hold it back. Sometimes, she could hear a tiny inner voice saying, "Please don't bite me! I want to grow long and beautiful."

After a while, Candy liked her red fingernails so much she stopped biting the other ones so that Dr. Dan would paint them red also. Soon all of her nails were painted her favorite color, and her hands looked very pretty. Candy, like Cory, had learned to control what she never knew she could. It felt wonderful.

# Molly Macaw

Molly was a macaw from the Amazon rainforest in Peru. A macaw is a kind of parrot—actually, the biggest and most beautiful member of the parrot family. Molly's feathers were the colors of a rainbow: blue, green, red, orange, and yellow. She was brought to the Ashland Zoo in the United States so everyone could see her beautiful rainbow feathers.

In the United States, everyone was kind to Molly, and she liked the zoo, but she missed the tropical forest in Peru with its tall trees and beautiful flowers, and she missed her friends. Molly had many good friends who lived with her near the wide Amazon River. There were frogs, monkeys, sloths, butterflies, snakes and lizards. Her best friend was a toucan. He had a big colorful beak that was perfect for tearing open fruit to eat.

One day, when Molly was feeling homesick, she pulled out one of her tail feathers. It seemed to make her feel better. The next day she pulled out two more. Soon, she got to be so good at pulling out her feathers that

she did it even when she wasn't feeling sad. Pulling out her feathers became a habit, something she did so easily she often didn't even know she was doing it.

There were other things that Molly did so well that she didn't even have to think about it—flying, for instance. That was a good habit.

Molly loved to fly to her favorite place—a small lake in the middle of the Ashland Zoo. One day, when she was perched on a tree there, she looked down and saw her reflection in the water.

"My feathers!" the macaw cried. "What happened to my beautiful feathers?"

Molly's coat of rainbow feathers was torn and ragged. Most of the red feathers—her favorite ones—were gone. Molly felt very upset. To soothe her feelings, she dipped her beak under her wing and pulled out a long, blue feather.

"Oh, no!" she squawked. "I didn't mean to do that. I've got to stop, but I don't know how."

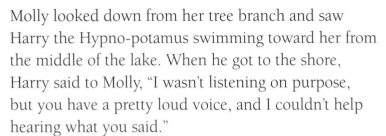

"I can help," said a cheerful voice.

Molly looked down from her tree branch and saw Harry the Hypno-potamus swimming toward her from the middle of the lake. When he got to the shore, Harry said to Molly, "I wasn't listening on purpose, but you have a pretty loud voice, and I couldn't help hearing what you said."

Molly was so startled she didn't know what to say.

"Dr. Dan, the veterinarian here at the zoo, showed me how I can control things I never knew I could by using my imagination," said Harry. "Dr. Dan calls it 'hypnosis.' I'm very good at it. That's why the sign over my new home says, 'Harry the Hypno-potamus.'"

"I sure could use some help," said Molly. "If I don't stop pulling out my feathers, I'll be as bald as a bird's egg. Do you think I could learn hypnosis?"

"Of course," said Harry. "Hypnosis is a lot like daydreaming on purpose. It is a way of thinking that helps you to help yourself. You can start right now."

Molly settled back on her tree branch and made herself comfortable.

"Imagine soaring through the rainforest," said Harry. "Notice all the shades of color … Listen to the sounds of the place—the birds, the monkeys, the insects, so familiar, so **safe**, so **comfortable** … Feel the warmth of the sun and the gentle coolness of a breeze on your feathers … Breathe in the smell of the place, so **relaxing**, so **peaceful** … Perhaps you are tasting your favorite food from the rainforest."

While Molly was using her imagination to see, feel, and hear her beautiful rainforest, and to eat its delicious fruit, she began to notice how **good** and how **comfortable** her body felt.

"I'm going to show Shurcan how to daydream on purpose," Molly said. "Shurcan is a toucan, but not a real one. I imagined him, just like I imagine soaring through the rainforest. But he is my friend, and he came all the way from the rainforest to keep me company."

"I bet Shurcan could help you to keep your feathers," said Harry. "Every time you feel the urge to pull out a feather, see and feel Shurcan Toucan's big, beautiful beak pushing your bill away from your feathers."

Molly closed her eyes and imagined.

"Sometimes," suggested Harry, "when you feel the urge to pull a feather, you could imagine finding a giant switch, like the kind that turns a light on and off. You could use that switch to turn off the urge to pull a feather. At other times when you feel like pulling your feathers, you could see a giant stop sign in your imagination."

Molly did all the things that Harry suggested. Then Harry said, "Look into the mirror of your imagination and see yourself as you would like to look, and feel, and be, with all of your pretty and colorful feathers."

"That's easy," said Molly. She looked into the mirror of her imagination every day, and her imaginary feathers grew prettier and more colorful all the time.

One day, when Molly flew to her favorite tree by the lake, she looked down from her branch and noticed her reflection. "My feathers really are thick and beautiful," Molly cried. "And see how long my tail feathers have grown!"

Every time that Molly used hypnosis to help herself with the habit she used to have, she felt very happy and proud at what she had been able to accomplish. She learned what she never knew she knew, and controlled what she never knew she could. She was thinking to help herself, daydreaming on purpose. She told all this to Harry the next time she saw him. Harry gave her a great big hippo grin.

"That's hypnosis," Harry said happily.

"I call it the Magic of Imagination," Molly Macaw said.

# Ol'Ness Bunny

One afternoon, when Harry the Hypno-potamus was taking a bath, he heard a scratching sound on the fence surrounding his mud puddle. It was a small sound, not much louder than a rustle, so the hippo didn't pay it much attention. He went on blowing bubbles in the mud and daydreaming. The sound got louder: scritch, scritch, scratch, scratch, sniffle. Someone was crying!

As he turned his head in the direction of the noise, Harry spied a rabbit crouching next to his fence. The bunny was not much longer than one of Harry's feet, and it was sobbing. The creature had soft fur the color of peanut butter, and floppy ears. Instead of standing up straight, as most rabbit ears do, those ears hung all the way down to the ground.

Harry rose from his bath and waddled over to the fence.

"Why, it's my old friend Ol'Ness, the lop-eared bunny!" he exclaimed. "Ol'Ness, whatever is wrong?"

Ol'Ness's nose trembled, her ears shivered like leaves in the wind, and her whiskers twitched. Harry knew that his friend was a worrier. Instead of her real name, which was Agnes, her five younger brothers and sisters called her "Ol'Ness." Like an old, old bunny, Ol'Ness worried and fretted about everything.

Ol'Ness worried about things that other bunnies never thought twice about. One sunny day, when the lop-eared rabbit hopped over to the zoo fence to visit Harry, she kept looking up and sniffing the wind.

"Dear me, Harry," she said, "I came all the way to the zoo without my umbrella. What if it rains?"

"There isn't a cloud in the sky," said Harry.

"Well, you know how clouds are," said Ol'Ness. "They come and go, come and go, all day long. You never know when a big, black thunderstorm cloud is going to come along."

On another day, Harry said to Ol'Ness, "You look especially bright-eyed today, my friend. Fit as a fiddle, I should say."

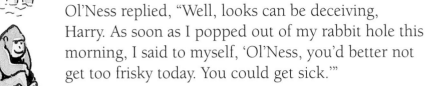

Ol'Ness replied, "Well, looks can be deceiving, Harry. As soon as I popped out of my rabbit hole this morning, I said to myself, 'Ol'Ness, you'd better not get too frisky today. You could get sick.'"

All this worry made Ol'Ness very nervous. After a while, her nose began to twitch, then her ears, and finally her whiskers. Now, today, with her friend the hippo staring at her with great concern, Ol'Ness continued to weep.

"Oh, Harry," she sniffled, dabbing at her tears with one of her long, soft ears, "it's just awful! I don't know what to do! Tomorrow I'm going to school for the very first time."

"Why, that's exciting, Ol'Ness," Harry said.

Ol'Ness gave a little scream. If you have ever heard a rabbit scream, you know it is a very scary sound—like a baby crying.

"What if I don't do good in bunny school?" she worried. "My brothers and sisters and everybody will laugh at me." The bunny's ears and nose and whiskers twitched furiously. "What if nobody likes me? They might not, especially now, when I've got all these tics."

Harry frowned, a great big hippo frown that wrinkled all of his forehead.

"A tic? What's that?" he asked.

Ol'Ness was so upset she could hardly answer. "It's this," she said, pointing to her quivering nose. "And this," she said, shaking her trembling ears.

"Ol'Ness," said Harry, "I know a way that you can help yourself."

The little rabbit stopped crying. "Really and truly?"

"Yes," said Harry. You can help yourself with hypnosis and the power of your imagination."

"That would be great," said Ol'Ness.

"First, you need to make yourself comfortable," Harry said.

Ol'Ness lay down on her tummy and stretched out her legs.

"Next," said Harry, "tighten all the muscles in your left back foot. Tight, tight, and then **relax**. That's right, very good, letting go. Now, tighten all the muscles in your right back foot, then **let go** of the tightness and **relax** even **more**. Tighten your left back leg and relax. Tighten your right back leg and relax. Tighten your hips, then let those muscles become **loose**, **limp**, and

**relaxed**. Now, tighten all those tummy muscles and relax. Your back tight, and then relaxed even more. Tighten all the muscles in your left front paw, hold that, then **relax**. Now your right front paw. Relax deeper and deeper. Tighten your left front leg and relax even **deeper**. Now your right front leg, and relax even **deeper**. Good. That's right. Tighten all those muscles in your face, your nose, your whiskers, your ears, and then relax, deeper and deeper, that wave of relaxation making you comfortable, relaxed and **calm**. All your muscles are loose, limp and **relaxed**."

As Ol' Ness lay stretched out, so relaxed and comfortable, Harry said, "Perhaps you would like to move the twitch from your face, where all the other bunnies can see it, all the way **down** to the little finger on your left front paw. There it can twitch as much as it wants or needs to."

Harry added, "Or you may decide to save the tic until later, when you are all by yourself, and none of the other bunnies are around, and then let it twitch.

"Imagine the urge to twitch which you would feel just before you twitch, and when you feel the urge, imagine a yellow traffic light that slows down the time between the urge to twitch and the twitch. Good," said Harry. "Now see the light change to red, stopping the twitch entirely."

Then Harry said, "Imagine taking a journey through your body and finding the twitch switch. I'm not sure if your twitch switch is an on–off switch, or more like a dimmer switch. Let your head nod to signal me when you have found it."

Harry noticed Ol'Ness's head nod. "Good. Is it an on–off switch, or a dimmer switch?"

Ol'Ness said it was a dimmer switch.

Harry said, "Then it would be alright to turn it down, way down."

"Imagine looking into the mirror of the future," Harry said. "Imagine seeing your cute little bunny face and lop ears still and calm, free of tics and twitches."

Ol'Ness did everything that Harry suggested, and it did make her feel more still and calm, from the tip of her whiskers all the way down to her fluffy tail. It also made her feel happy and proud that she was the boss of her twitches.

Every night at bedtime, Ol'Ness practiced relaxing all her muscles. She liked to imagine being at the top of a mountain where the wind was blowing, and making

all the leaves twitch and twitter on their stems, and then hopping **down** a path **down** the mountain. She noticed, as she went **down**, that the wind was blowing less and less, and the leaves were **even more quiet** and **still** as she continued **down** the mountain to a place of **stillness** and **calm**.

"I love hypnosis," said Ol'Ness.

Harry smiled a great big hippo grin that started in his bright little eyes and slid all the way down his round, gray body, right down to his broad, strong, hippopotamus feet.

He said, "I wonder how wonderful it would be to discover in how many different places, and in how many different ways, you could use hypnosis to help yourself."

"If I start using hypnosis like that," said Ol'Ness, "everybody will have to stop calling me 'Ol'Ness'. My name will be 'Hypno-rabbit', instead."

# Voit Zebra

Voit was not sure which color he liked best: black or white. That's because Voit himself was half black and half white. He was a zebra. No two zebras are exactly alike. Each zebra has stripes that are arranged in a different pattern. In Africa, where Voit was born, zebras are one of the lions' favorite meals. Zebras always live and move around in large groups. That way, when they are standing together, their stripes blend into one big pattern. This makes it hard for a lion to pick out just one animal to attack. Even so, living in Africa made Voit nervous.

Voit was not sure how or why it got started, but at some point, when he was younger, and still living in Africa, he started to grind his teeth and clench his jaw. He got very good at it because he did it so much. Later, when Voit and his family moved to the Ashland Zoo, and didn't have to worry about getting eaten, Voit continued to grind and clench his teeth without even thinking about it. Sometimes, he even did it in his sleep. All that clenching gave him a headache and made his cheeks ache.

Voit's mother worried about all this clenching and grinding, so she took Voit to see Dr. Kay, the zoo dentist.

"Grinding is not good for your teeth," Dr. Kay told Voit. "I can show you how to help yourself to stop," the dentist said. "I can help you to learn how to do self-hypnosis so that you can control what you never knew you could."

Dr. Kay suggested, "Imagine stepping into a pond of warm relaxing water. Feel how **comfortable** your feet are. Then, going **deeper**, your legs **relaxed**, your muscles lose and limp, go **even deeper** yet, that relaxation going up to your hips, and then your chest, that relaxation going into your neck as you go **deeper** and **deeper**, your muscles smooth, **relaxed** and at ease. Since, in your imagination, you can do anything, you can even breathe under water as your head and face are surrounded by the **comfort** of the warm water. Your cheeks and jaw are **relaxed** and **comfortable**. That's right, **deeply** relaxed."

Dr. Kay said, " You may wish to imagine delicious, thick, soothing honey being pored over the top of your head, slowly drifting **down** over your forehead, your eyelids very **heavy** and **relaxed** and comfortable, that flow of **comfort** slowly coating your cheeks and jaw. All the muscles of your face are loose, limp, and **relaxed**. That's right, very **comfortable**, and your jaw relaxing **even more** now. Good. Very good."

"In the future," said Dr. Kay, "any time you begin to feel the urge to grind or clench, you may be surprised to notice just the beginning of a yawn as your jaw **relaxes** and drops **down** slightly, then more and **more relaxed**."

Dr. Kay told Voit the story of another zebra that she knew named Jody. One day, when Jody was yawning a very big yawn, a tiny baby bird, who was just learning to fly, flitted right into the zebra's mouth. The baby bird's mother was very upset.

The baby bird's nest was way over on the other side of the field. Jody didn't want to hurt the baby bird, and she didn't want her to get trampled by the other zebras. She decided that the safest and best way to get the baby back to her nest and her mother was to carry it safely across the field in her mouth.

With her lips closed so the little bird wouldn't fall out, Jody made room in her mouth for the little bird. She imagined holding a bucket of sand with her lower jaw, pulling down, while a helium balloon was attached to her upper jaw, pulling up. Meanwhile, Jody held her lips together, making room for the little bird inside her mouth. When she reached the other side of the field, the zebra gently parted her lips, allowing the baby bird to join her sisters and brothers in the nest. Jody felt very proud that she was able to create enough comfortable space in her mouth for the tiny bird just by using her imagination.

Voit knew that he could solve the problem he used to have all by himself, just by using his imagination. Once he solved his problem, the zebra could turn his attention to important things, such as: was he black with white stripes or white with black stripes?

# Sugar Man Meerkat

Sugar Man was a meerkat. These little creatures are members of the mongoose family, and they don't look at all like cats. Like weasels or ferrets, they have long, slender bodies, and long tails. Sugar Man and his big, extended family—even his uncles and aunts and cousins—came to the Ashland Zoo from the Kalahari Desert in southern Africa. Because they like to stand on their hind feet, meerkats are known in the Spanish language as "little men of the desert."

Meerkats live in large family groups of about 40, and they are very good at cooperating and working together. Sugar Man's mother looked for food such as beetles, scorpions, and small reptiles, while his father, who was about twelve inches long, stood up on his back legs to guard his family. He watched for any predators such as eagles and cobras. Meerkats have very sharp eyes that can spot an eagle 1,000 feet away. If one of these animals came near, Sugar Man's father would fight fiercely to defend his family. Other members of this large family provided daycare for Sugar Man and the other young meerkats.

In the desert it gets very cold at night, so all the meerkats slept together in one big furry pile. That was a problem for Sugar Man because he still wet the bed. He worried about this, and one day he told his friend Harry the Hypno-potamus all about it.

"Maybe Dr. Dan, the zoo veterinarian, could help you," said Harry.

"I'll go see him right away," Sugar Man said.

Dr Dan explained to Sugar Man how his brain and bladder worked perfectly all day long. "Your kidneys make urine—that's what you like to call 'pee,'" said Dr. Dan. "The pee travels through tubes into your bladder. When your bladder gets full, it sends a message to your brain that you need to get outside to let the pee come out. Until you are in the place where you need to be in order to pee, your brain sends a message to the muscle in your bladder to stay tight and hold the pee inside. Then, when you are ready, your brain tells your bladder muscle to relax and let the pee out."

"There are 1,440 minutes in a day," Dr. Dan told Sugar Man. "For 1,439 of those minutes, your brain and bladder work together just right. Then, for some reason, for one minute during the night, something goes wrong with the signals sent back and forth between your brain and bladder."

Dr. Dan continued, "Your brain is like a computer. The computer has different programs that tell your body what to do. You can change these programs."

Sugar Man imagined the computer in his brain. He programmed the signals between his brain and bladder for success. He programmed his computer for dry nights every night.

Sugar Man made sure that all the circuits, from his bladder to his brain and back again, were working just right. When his bladder got full, it sent the message to his brain. His brain sent back the message to the muscle that holds the pee in, to stay tight, tight, tight through the night, night, night. Sugar Man also made sure the computer in his brain had a back-up plan. Sometimes, when his bladder sent the message to his brain, his brain would wake him up so he could go outside to the meerkat toilet to pee.

Meerkats live as a cooperative society, where everyone helps each other. Some of the meerkats decided to remind Sugar Man to have only one glass of milk with dinner. Other meerkats said they would help Sugar Man remember to pee before bedtime.

Sugar Man told them, "Thanks for wanting to help me, but it is my problem, and I am going to be the boss of my pee myself."

Sugar Man drank all the milk and water he wanted during the day, but he only had one glass of milk at dinner. After that, he didn't drink any more. Every night, Sugar Man peed before joining his family in the furry pile. He imagined the computer in his brain working just right. As his bladder got fuller, it sent a message to his brain. The brain sent a message back to the muscle in the bladder to stay tight through the night. Sugar Man imagined waking up dry in his furry pile of meerkats. How good that made him feel! It also made all the other meerkats in that dry, furry pile feel good and happy.

As he fell asleep, Sugar Man repeated over and over, "Tight, tight, tight through the night, night, night."

Sugar Man kept a calendar so he could show Dr. Dan all his dry nights. Looking at his calendar reminded Sugar Man how good he was at being the boss of his

98

pee. Every morning when Sugar Man woke up dry, he put a smiley face on the calendar. Soon, day after day was a smiley face. That put a very big smile on Sugar Man's face. He liked being the boss of his pee. All the other meerkats who slept in the furry pile that now was always dry, were also happy that Sugar Man was the boss of his pee.

Sugar Man solved the problem he used to have by himself, just by using hypnosis and the power of his own imagination.

# Lonnie Llama

Lonnie was a young llama who lived at the Ashland Zoo with her parents and many other llamas. Llamas come from South America. Like their close relatives, the camels, llamas are very strong, and they are used to carrying heavy loads. Llamas have thick wool, like sheep, but their necks and their ears are long. They are curious, shy, and gentle, but they can also be very stubborn.

The llamas at the Ashland Zoo lived together in a large field enclosed by a wire fence. At night, when it was raining or very cold, the llamas stayed together in a shelter. The shelter had a roof and walls, like a house.

Llamas keep themselves and their surroundings very clean. They only poop in one place. All the llamas at Ashland had chosen to poop in a back corner of their enclosure. When Lonnie was very small, her mother showed her where she was supposed to poop. Lonnie didn't like to go in that corner. She liked to go right behind the shelter, and squat with her tail hanging down. Often some of the poop got on her tail.

No one, especially her parents, wanted Lonnie to

poop right behind the shelter. They wanted her to put her poops where all the other llamas put theirs. Her mother and father were tired of cleaning the poop off her tail. They wished she would poop in the same place, and in the same way, as everybody else.

Lonnie didn't want to disappoint her parents, but she really didn't like to poop where all the other llamas went. Instead, she decided not to poop at all. She held her poop in her tummy and wouldn't let it come out. That gave her a tummy ache. Finally, she couldn't hold it in anymore—her tummy hurt too much—so she pooped. Because she had kept them in her tummy so long, the poops were big and hard, and it hurt to push them out.

Lonnie was just a little llama, so she didn't understand that it is a good thing to poop every day. She didn't like to poop where all the other llamas pooped, and it hurt when she had big, hard poops. She didn't want to make her parents sad by going right behind the shelter and getting poop on her tail, so she decided that she was definitely NOT going to poop anymore. She

101

would hold the poop in her tummy. It was a big job to hold such a lot of poop in her tummy, and it gave Lonnie a big tummy ache. Sometimes, some poop just snuck out without Lonnie ever knowing about it. The poop got all over her tail, and it made her smell stinky. Some of the other young llamas teased her.

When Lonnie got much older, holding her poop in had become a habit, something she did so much that she didn't even need to think about it. All that poop did, however, give her a tummy ache most of the time. Lonnie didn't like it when the other animals called her "Stinky" because loose poop was always sneaking out and getting all over her tail.

Dr. Dan was the veterinarian at the zoo. When he heard that Lonnie had a tummy ache, and that her poop was sneaking out all day, he came to see her. Dr. Dan talked to Lonnie for a long time, and gave her a very careful examination. Lonnie's parents told Dr. Dan that they thought Lonnie had diarrhea because her poop was always sneaking out all over her tail. Dr. Dan told Lonnie and her mother and father that actually Lonnie was very constipated. That meant that she had a tummy full of poop that needed to come out. Lonnie had been holding her poop inside for so long, and so much, that it stretched out her intestines.

(The intestines are part of a long digestive tube that carries food from the mouth into the stomach to be digested. The leftover waste moves through the intestines and comes out through the anus. The anus is the opening on the backside where the poop comes out.)

"Would you like to learn about hypnosis and how to be the boss of your poops?" Dr. Dan asked Lonnie.

"That sounds great," Lonnie said.

"Why don't you go someplace wonderful in your imagination," Dr. Dan suggested, "some place that's fun, and makes you feel **safe** and **secure**."

Lonnie liked to play soccer. She was very good at soccer, so she imagined playing in a soccer game. Lonnie noticed that when the ball was at the other end of the field, the goalie was relaxed. Then, as Lonnie brought the ball downfield, the goalie became more alert, not wanting to let anything get by. Lonnie knew just what to do: all her muscles working perfectly, she put the ball right into the goal.

Dr. Dan told Lonnie, "To help make your poops softer, it is very important for you to drink lots of water, to eat lots of vegetables, and to take some medicine for a while. Part of being the boss of your poops means

that if you have an accident, it is your responsibility to clean it up and wash your tail off."

The next thing they needed to do, according to Dr. Dan, was to get all the old, hard, dry poops out of Lonnie's tummy. Lonnie's mother squirted some special water up through Lonnie's anus into her intestines to soften up the poop and help it come out. This was called an "enema." At first, Lonnie didn't like it very much. Then, she discovered that she could return to the soccer field in her imagination, and the enema no longer bothered her. She imagined putting the soccer ball right where it needed to go. She was very good at moving the ball down the field, then waiting for just the right moment to put it right in the goal.

Dr. Dan told Lonnie a story about a boat that was traveling down a long, winding river: "As the boat got closer to where the river flows out to sea, the boat noticed that a few other boats had stopped. There was a bridge across the river, and the boats were too big to pass underneath. This bridge, though, was special. It was called a 'drawbridge.' Every morning and every night, the bridge was raised up so the boats could go through out to the ocean. The boat watched as the boss of the drawbridge gave the signal to raise

the bridge at just the right moment, and all the boats sailed easily out to sea."

Every day, after breakfast and after supper, Lonnie went to the back corner where all the llamas pooped. She sat there for ten minutes so she could poop. While she sat there, Lonnie used her imagination to think of something special, something wonderful. Using her imagination made her feel comfortable and relaxed. She liked to imagine scoring three goals in one game. This is called a "hat trick." She noticed how well all her muscles worked together, like a team. She imagined that she was the team captain. Even when Lonnie didn't poop after breakfast or after supper, Dr. Dan suggested that she could feel very proud just for sitting there and noticing how loose and relaxed all her muscles felt.

Soon, Lonnie realized that being the boss of her poops was easier than she ever thought it would be, and fun, too. It felt wonderful not to have tummy aches anymore. Every time she pooped in the back corner where all the other llamas pooped, she put a star on her calendar. Everyone was so proud that Lonnie was the boss of her poops. The first week, she got three stars in one week. She told Dr. Dan that it was a "hat trick." To celebrate, Dr. Dan got her a great big hat.

# Davey Manatee

Davey was a kind of sea cow called a manatee. He had flippers like a seal, and a tail that was shaped like a giant spoon. Davey lived in the rivers of Florida, where he spent most of his day eating all the plants that grew on the bottom of the river. He could eat 100 pounds of river plants in just one day. By munching on weeds that grow in the water, manatees keep the rivers clear so that motorboats can travel on them.

Manatees are not fish; they are mammals. They need air to breathe. Davey could stay underwater for 15 minutes. One day, when he was coming up to the surface to get a breath of air, he bumped into the propeller of a motorboat and got several very big cuts.

Some game wardens took Davey to the animal hospital. The hospital called Dr. Thom, who was the veterinary surgeon at the Ashland Zoo.

"We've got an injured manatee here," the people at the hospital told Dr. Thom. "We need you to come sew him up."

When Dr. Thom arrived, Davey was crying because his cuts were bleeding, and they hurt a lot.

"Wow!" said Dr. Thom when he saw Davey. "You have got great lungs, and big beautiful tears, and look at that healthy, red blood! Isn't it wonderful that your body knew just what to do to wash the germs away with your bright, red, blood. What a great job it is doing! Your blood even has special cells—we call them killer cells—to fight off any germs. Soon, your cuts will begin to bleed a little less until the bleeding stops. I wonder which cut will stop bleeding first?"

Dr. Thom noticed that Davey's eyes were very big and round as he looked around at all the things in the hospital.

The surgeon said, "I work at the hospital almost every day, so I am very used to all the stuff we have here, but I know it can be a little scary for you. You may hear different noises, or see strange-looking things, or smell unusual smells. If you wonder what it is, or how we use it, just ask me, and I will tell you. All the equipment we have in the hospital helps us to help you stay safe and get better quickly."

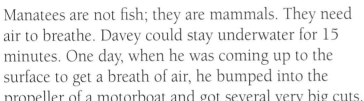

Dr. Thom and a nurse named Mary got everything ready to sew up Davey's cuts so he could start healing immediately. Dr. Thom explained that he was going to put some medicine in and around the cut so that it would be completely numb when he sewed it up. He asked Davey if he would like to practice his "ouch."

"Could I hear your best 'ouch?'" asked Dr. Thom.

Davey said, "**Ouch**."

"Could I hear an even bigger 'ouch?'"

## "OUCH."

"Any bigger than that?"

## "OUCH!"

"How about your biggest 'ouch?'"

## "OUCH!!"

"Oh," said Dr. Thom, "that would be perfect if you ever broke your flipper, but you are not going to need that big an ouch, probably just a tiny ouch like this: 'ouch.' You can say any size ouch you want or need to, but you will probably only need that little ouch. Some people say it feels like a little mosquito bite when I put the numbing medicine in. I wonder what it will feel like to you, and how little it needs to bother you."

Mary asked Davey, "Where would you rather be instead of here in the emergency room at the hospital getting stitched up?"

Davey said, "I'd rather be at the bottom of the river. I like to watch the crayfish swim backwards. They can swim backwards very fast, and they like to hang out near the water lily roots, which are one of my very favorite things to eat."

Mary suggested, "You could go there in your imagination, and chase the crayfish at the bottom of the river, and taste the yummy water lily roots in your mouth."

Davey was having so much fun watching the crayfish and dining on roots in his imagination, that Dr. Thom finished stitching up the cuts, and Davey forgot all about using the "ouch" he had practiced. He would save the "ouch" until next time.

Then Davey thought, "I won't even need the 'ouch' next time, because I have my imagination. I can chase crayfish backwards instead."

Dr. Thom and Mary told Davey that it would be all right to feel very proud.

# Handel Tapir

When Voit, the zebra, first saw Handel, he thought he was a very funny-looking, short, fat zebra, because he had stripes just like Voit's. Molly Macaw, who came from a rainforest in South America just like Handel did, knew that Handel wasn't a zebra. He was a tapir—a stout animal with a long snout, like a pig's. When he got older, Handel would lose his stripes.

While he was still living in Peru, Handel got his back leg caught in a trap. The doctors were able to save a portion of his leg, but the tapir was always in pain. He was sent to the Ashland Zoo so that Dr. Dan, the veterinarian, could teach him how to use hypnosis.

The first time that Handel limped into the veterinarian's office, Dr. Dan explained, "Hypnosis is a way of thinking certain thoughts on purpose. You can use it to help yourself with your pain." Then he suggested that Handel get comfortable. Handel lay down on his back so he could rest his injured leg.

"Imagine that there is a magnet on each of your front hooves," said Dr. Dan.

In his mind, Handel saw a picture of a strong iron magnet attached to each of his front hooves.

"Imagine the magnets pulling your hooves together," said Dr. Dan, "pulling them gently together, a little at first, and then more and more. Concentrate on the sensation of the magnet pulling your hooves together."

While Dr. Dan said this, Handel felt his hooves moving slowly toward each other.

"As your hooves get closer and closer together," said Dr. Dan, "perhaps you will notice that you are getting **more** and more **relaxed**, **more** and more **comfortable**. When your hooves meet, your eyes will **close**, and you will be very **deeply** relaxed."

When Handel's hooves moved closer and touched each other, Handel's eyelids slowly closed, and his whole body felt sleepy and relaxed.

"Now, imagine a big, beautiful package," said Dr. Dan. "The card on the present is addressed to you. On the top of the colorful package there is a big, bright bow. Go ahead and open the gift. Inside is a **comfort**

cloak. The cloak's color is so beautiful, so **soothing**. It is the color of **comfort**. The card that came with the package says that any time you have less comfort than you need, you can open your present and cover yourself with the invisible cloak of **comfort**. Notice how **good** it makes your entire body feel to be cloaked in **comfort**. Your shoulders, your back, your tummy, your legs, all wrapped in **comfort**. You can unwrap that package of **comfort** whenever and wherever you want or need to. It is a present you give yourself, a cloak of **comfort**."

While Handel was still wrapped in his soothing comfort cloak, Dr. Dan asked him to imagine two big television screens side by side.

"On one screen there is a movie of Handel feeling very uncomfortable," said Dr. Dan. "On the other screen there is a movie of Handel feeling happy, comfortable, and good.

"Pretend that you have two very special remote controls in your hooves. I'm not sure how you will do this, or what you will do first, but using the remotes you have in each hoof, make the happy screen bigger."

In Handel's mind, the magnets on each of his front hooves turned into TV remotes. Gently, he pressed his right hoof against the floor. The happy screen grew bigger.

"Now make the happy screen even bigger," said Dr. Dan.

Again, Handel pressed his right hoof against the floor. The happy screen grew big, big, big.

"Good," said Dr. Dan, "now make the other screen, where you are uncomfortable, a little smaller."

Handel pressed his left hoof against the floor.

"Even smaller yet," said Dr. Dan.

Again Handel pressed his left hoof against the floor.

"Great!" said Dr. Dan. "As the screen gets smaller, you may be surprised to notice the volume getting softer and softer. That's right. Now, turn it down until you can barely see or hear it. Notice how **good** you feel, both here in the room, and also on the big, happy TV screen. The big, happy screen just continues to get bigger until it almost fills your whole imagination, doesn't it **now** … Let me know when the uncomfortable one is all gone. Good. Now you can just take a few moments to **enjoy** the happy, big screen TV."

Handel lay quietly, enjoying the picture on his big, happy TV screen. In his mind, he saw a picture of the rainforest. Handel and his brothers and sisters were all playing happily together.

"In the future," said Dr. Dan, "any time you are beginning to feel any discomfort, you may choose to watch it on TV. You can turn down the volume like you just did, or perhaps you will just change the channel. You can feel very **proud** that you were able to **control** your level of **comfort** by yourself."

"There is another place that you might like to go in your imagination," said Dr. Dan. "You might like to find the time machine room. In this place, there are magic buttons that can speed up time or slow it **down, way down**. When you press one of the buttons, it will speed up your time of discomfort so that it will go by fast. The other button will slow down your time of **comfort**, so that **feeling good** and comfortable will last for a very **long time**."

"Is there any reason, big or small, good or silly, that you should not stop letting the pain bother you?" asked Dr. Dan. "Is there anything you will miss about the pain when it is gone?"

Handel let his head nod back and forth, saying "no" to both questions.

"Good," said Dr. Dan "Now it will be all right to turn the calendar ahead. I'm not sure if it will be tomorrow, or next week, that you will notice how good you have been feeling. Things will be different: a little, or a lot, or maybe in-between. The more you see things the way you want them to be, the more they can be, because you can make them just that way in your imagination. Each day, and in every way, you will find yourself feeling better and better about what you were able to accomplish by yourself."

Even though Handel would always have a problem with his leg, he had learned some ways to help himself with the pain. The discomfort no longer needed to bother him so much, and that made him a very happy tapir.

112

# Julie Giraffe

When Julie was born, she was already over six feet tall. In the next few years, she would grow another eight feet. She would be almost as tall as her dad, who was seventeen feet tall, and the tallest land mammal—a giraffe.

Julie and her family came to the Ashland Zoo from the plains of sub-Saharan Africa. All of their coats were marked with patterns that looked like a jigsaw puzzle. The family liked to eat shrubs, vines and leaves. Even when the leaves grew on trees that had big, sharp thorns, Julie's long, flexible tongue enabled her to eat without getting pricked.

The young giraffe had a very large and loving heart. When she was full-grown, her heart would weigh as much as twenty-four pounds. She needed that big heart to pump her blood all the way up through her long neck to her head.

When Julie wanted a drink, the pond was a long way down. To get closer, she had to spread her front feet wide apart. When the giraffe lowered her head, a complicated system of valves, like tiny gates, slowed down the flow of blood through Julie's long neck to her brain. If the blood ran through the veins in her neck too quickly, Julie would feel as if her head were going to burst. One of Julie's valves didn't work just right, so she often got headaches.

One day, when Julie was leaning over the pond, her friend, Harry the Hypno-potamus, swam up. Julie dipped her head to greet him. Her movement was so quick that her weak valve did not have time to help her blood slow down. Julie's head began to ache, and her big, brown eyes closed in pain.

"What's wrong?" asked Harry.

Julie told him about her headaches.

"Maybe Dr. Dan, the zoo veterinarian, can help," said Harry. "He helped me many times. I go right by his office on my way home. I'll take you there."

When they got to Dr. Dan's office, the veterinarian talked to Julie and checked her over very carefully. "I can teach you a way to help yourself," he said. "You can do it with self-hypnosis."

"It's a lot of fun," said Harry, who had stayed around in case Julie needed him.

"Close your eyes," Dr. Dan told Julie. "Imagine that you are flying on a magic carpet. The carpet takes you up into the clouds to a magical place. Pegasus, the flying horse with wings, is there, and unicorns, and butterflies as big as watermelons. There are also lots of juicy leaves to eat, and there is music and dancing."

Julie had so much fun in that magical place that she forgot all about the headache she used to have.

"Sometimes," said Dr. Dan, "instead of taking an imaginary trip on the magic carpet and leaving your headache behind, you will decide to stay right where you are, and send the headache off to someplace else. Perhaps you will chose to attach the headache to a helium balloon, and watch it float higher and farther away until it is just a spot on the horizon. In place of the headache is a **large amount of comfort**. You can get to know this place of comfort, and watch it expand and grow, as the **place of comfort** gets bigger and **bigger**, and the **time of comfort** gets longer and **longer**, until you can forget to remember, or remember to forget, the headache you used to have."

"At some time, if you have a headache, you might decide that you would like to move it to someplace less bothersome. Perhaps, even now, you can feel it moving **down** to your left front foot. As it moves, you will notice another interesting thing beginning **now**, the headache changing from a pounding to a slight banging as it moves down, **down** into your left foot, then, changing even more to a little tapping that does not need to bother or disturb you, changing as it goes down, **down** into your foot, bothering less and less, going **down**. That's right, just a slight tapping now in your left foot."

On another day when Julie went to see Dr. Dan, he asked, "What color is your headache?"

"Red," Julie said.

"You will be happy to discover," said Dr. Dan, "how you can change the color of your headaches to one of **comfort**, and how **good** that will make you feel."

Julie imagined the color of her headache, and then watched it change from red to orange to yellow to green to blue to purple. Purple was her color of comfort.

"Pain is neither good nor bad, but it is important," Dr. Dan told Julie. "It is a lot like a smoke detector. A smoke alarm can be very annoying when it goes off,

but it is necessary. It can warn you of a fire. After you have done what needs to be done to check for smoke or put out the fire, then it would be okay to turn the smoke detector down."

Dr. Dan asked Julie to give her headache a number on a scale of zero to ten. "Zero would be no headache, and ten would be the worst headache you could imagine," he said.

"My headache is a seven," Julie answered.

Dr. Dan said, "I wonder if you have ever noticed that sometimes, when all you are doing is thinking about the ache in your head, you can increase the discomfort of your headache to an eight or nine. I wonder how wonderful it will be for you, **now** that you will have a way to **decrease** those numbers, to dial those headache numbers **down**, going **down** like dominoes falling in slow motion, going **down, down** to the level that is **comfortable** for you. Go ahead and do that **now**, dialing the headache **down**, the numbers getting **smaller**, the headache less and **less**. It will be exciting to see how **low** it will go. Then it would be all right to feel very **proud** that you were able to solve the problem with headaches that you **used** to have, all by yourself, just by using hypnosis and the power of your imagination."

That night, when Julie went to sleep, she had many happy dreams. She dreamed of magic carpets, of purple clouds, and a big, soft place of comfort, where she floated away her headaches on a helium balloon.

116

# Milton Cheetah

It was nighttime at the Boo Hoo Zoo. Milton, the cheetah, felt angry and lonely and very, very hungry. Once again, the zookeepers had forgotten to bring his supper, just like they did almost every night.

Milton snarled and bit the bars of his cage with his long, sharp teeth. It didn't help. He couldn't get out of the cage, and he couldn't get his dinner. So he roared.

"ARRRRROARRR!"

The zookeepers came running, but they didn't bring any food. They yelled at Milton. They kicked him and pulled his tail. They slammed the door of his cage and left him all alone in the dark.

Before Milton came to the Boo Hoo Zoo, he lived in Africa with his mother and other cheetahs. These animals, which are cousins of lions and tigers, are the fastest animals on earth. They have beautiful reddish-brown coats spotted with soft black markings.

One day, when Milton was a little cub, hunters came to Milton's home on the grassland looking for animals with beautiful coats. They shot Milton's mother. They put Milton in a big box and shipped him to the Boo Hoo Zoo.

The Boo Hoo Zoo was a terrible place. The zookeepers, who were supposed to take good care of Milton, were mean to him. Their bad treatment made Milton feel both sad and mad. He was always losing his temper. He would growl and snarl. The other animals at Boo Hoo Zoo were afraid of Milton. Nobody wanted to be his friend.

One night, when Milton was alone in his cold, dark cage, he started to cry. It was a long, sad, lonely, hungry wail. Suddenly, the light in his cage went on. The zookeepers were coming! Milton was scared. A man entered his cage. He was a zookeeper Milton had never seen before. Ever so gently, the zookeeper lifted Milton from his cage and put him in a box with a deep, soft bed of clean straw. Milton hissed at him.

"Cheer up, old buddy," said the zookeeper. "We're going to the Ashland Zoo."

When Milton woke up the next morning, he was lying

on his soft straw bed in a cozy den. A man with white hair and a kind face was sitting beside him.

The man smiled at Milton and said, "Welcome to Ashland Zoo."

Milton snarled.

"We heard about how they were treating you over at Boo Hoo," said the man. "That's why we brought you here. I'm the zoo veterinarian. They call me Dr. Dan. I'm here to give you a check-up."

Milton growled at Dr. Dan and tried to bite his foot.

"I can tell that you are a very angry cheetah," said Dr. Dan. "On the outside you seem pretty healthy, but I'm worried that you are hurting on the inside. People who should have been good to you and were supposed to take care of you were mean to you."

A hot, salty tear squeezed from Milton's eye and ran down his beautiful, spotted cheek.

"Everybody feels angry sometimes," Dr. Dan told Milton. "When somebody annoys us or something makes us mad, we get upset. Some animals, like some humans, get angry over little things very fast. Others get angry very slowly, and it takes a lot to get them mad. Some animals can get over their anger quickly;

others take a long time. Some people, and even some animals, always seem to be angry. They hold onto their anger like a favorite pet, and they never let it go. The keepers at the Boo Hoo Zoo who didn't take good care of you were probably like that."

Milton listened carefully to everything that Dr. Dan told him. "I get angry very fast," he told Dr. Dan, "and I do feel that way a lot of the time."

"Anger it is normal," said Dr. Dan. "It isn't good or bad, but the way some people behave when they are angry can be bad. Some people keep their anger bottled up inside them and never tell anyone how upset they are. That can make them unhappy. Sometimes, it even makes them sick. Other people yell and scream; they throw things and break them, or they take their anger out on other people, just like the keepers at the Boo Hoo Zoo did to you. People like that make others angry."

Milton nodded sadly.

"It wasn't your fault that the zookeepers were angry, and you couldn't do anything about their angry, bad behavior," said Dr. Dan. "You are only responsible for dealing with your own anger and your own behavior."

Milton laid his head down between his paws. "I don't know how to do that," he said.

"I know something that can help you manage your angry feelings quickly and effectively," said Dr. Dan. "I've got a friend who's going to teach you hypnosis."

Milton lifted his head a little. "Hypnosis? What's that?"

Just then, a small woman with dark hair came into Milton's den.

"This is Zendi," said Dr. Dan. "She is a very special nurse, a nurse practitioner. She can help you deal with your temper."

Milton lifted his head up high. "That sounds great," he said. "I want the other animals at Ashland zoo to like me and be my friends."

Zendi sat down beside Milton. "I'm going to teach you how to do belly breathing," she said. "Sitting just the way you are now, take deep, relaxing breaths all the way **down, deep** in your belly, noticing how each slow breath makes you feel even **more relaxed** and comfortable. Breathe in **comfort** and breathe out stress, every breath taking you **deeper** and deeper **relaxed**."

As Milton did his belly breathing, his paws, which were squeezed into tight little fists, began to open and relax. Milton's jaws, which he shut so tightly that his teeth ached, opened wide in a sleepy yawn.

Zendi suggested, "It would be interesting for you to feel the angry feelings go **down** each time you breathe out. That's right, and with each breath **let go** of a little more anger, and then more and more, going **down**, with each breath, down **deeper**, letting go, perhaps noticing how all your muscles are **loose** and **relaxed** and **comfortable**."

"Now, while you are so nicely relaxed and comfortable," Zendi said softly, "go someplace wonderful in your imagination, a place so familiar and **safe**, so **peaceful**."

A warm spot of comfort grew and grew in Milton's chest. He felt like he was back home in Africa lying in the sunshine.

"Just take a moment to enjoy this special place," said Zendi. "That's right. Listen for the sounds of this place, so relaxing, so familiar. Breathe in the smells of peacefulness. Notice everything about this special place. This is a place that is always inside you. You can return to this place whenever and wherever you want

120

or need to, staying as long or as little as you would like. It is a gift you give yourself—a present that can be wrapped and unwrapped over and over. Each time you return to this place of comfort, it becomes easier and easier, and you can get there even more quickly. All you ever need to do, no matter where you are, or who you are with, is pay attention to your breathing. Breathing slowly, way **down deep** in your belly, letting every breath take you **deeper and deeper**, just breathing, will have a way of doing that. Then go someplace fun and safe in your imagination."

Milton did as Zendi suggested. In his imagination, he went back to the wide grassland in Africa where he had played as a cub.

"Now," said Zendi, "remember the angry feelings you used to have. Feel those angry feelings again. As you notice them, allow them to flow from your brain, down your arm, all the way down past your elbow, collecting in your paw. Wait till all your anger is there where you yourself put it. As you breath in, count to five as you crush that anger in your fist. Then, as you breathe out, throw the crushed-up, angry feelings away. Far away. I wonder how wonderful that will make you feel. Breathe in those good, happy, proud feelings."

Zendi said to Milton, "Imagine a big-screen television controlled by a remote control in your paw. On the screen you see a video of how you used to act, feel, and be when you were angry. Since you are in control of the remote, just like you are in control of your behavior, you can stop the video of your temper tantrum and bad behavior with the remote."

"Re-wind the tape to just before you started to get angry," Zendi suggested. "Watch it again in slow motion until the anger is over. Now, run it backwards, and stop it before it starts. Since, in your imagination, you can do anything you want, re-write the ending. Change it; re-write it from where you begin to get angry. See yourself doing something different. That's good …Yes … Much better. Notice with pride how good it feels to **be in control**. Pop that video out and keep it in a safe place so you can replay it whenever you want or need to. It's to remind yourself how you can **control** what you never knew you could."

"In the future," said Zendi, "anytime you are beginning to feel any angry feelings, you may choose to watch them on TV and just stop them, or change the channel. Then, it would be all right to feel very proud that you were able to control your anger and your temper by yourself. As you get better and better at it,

and like yourself even more, the other animals will like you, too, and want to be your friend."

Milton was so eager to get rid of his angry behavior and make new friends, he began right away to practice the things that Zendi taught him. He took walks all over the zoo, practicing his breathing all the time. One day, Milton was concentrating so hard on taking slow, deep breaths, that he didn't even see the mud puddle in front of him. He didn't see the hippo who was taking his mud bath. He didn't even notice the grin on the face of Harry the Hypno-potamus, who was going to be Milton's very first friend.

# Norma and Phil Beaver

Norma and Phil Beaver were the best engineers and builders in the Ashland Zoo. Their bodies were perfect for living life in the water. For one thing, the toes on their back feet were connected by webs, like duck feet. These webs helped them to paddle fast through the water. They also had flat tails that helped them to steer when they swam. When Phil stood up on his back legs to gnaw down a tree with his teeth, his tail held him up and helped him to keep his balance. Norma used her tail to smack down on the water. The sound warned other beavers, and scared enemies away.

Phil could hold his breath for 15 minutes underwater. Norma could swim for a half mile without having to come up for air. Beavers have two pairs of eyelids, one inside the other. When Norma and Phil closed their inner eyelids, it was like wearing goggles, or safety glasses, that allowed them to see better underwater. Their inner eyelids also protected their eyes against twigs when they were gnawing down trees in the forest.

Norma and Phil loved to cut down trees. Beavers' teeth continue to grow for all their lives. By gnawing on wood, beavers are able to keep their teeth from getting too long. Norma liked to eat bark and roots. Phil's favorite snacks were twigs and leaves. The beavers cut down tree branches, and used them to build dams and houses. The houses, which are called "lodges," look like Native American tepees in the water.

Beavers can create a big pond, or small lake, by building a dam across a stream. Using their paws and teeth, they lace the branches together and cement them with mud. They bring the mud up from the bottom of the lake by holding it against their chest with their paws.

Beavers can't see very well, so they depend on their hearing and sense of smell to let them know what is happening around them. More and more often, Phil thought that he could hear water running. The sound of running water could mean there was a hole in the dam. Even when the dam and the lodge were perfect, Phil couldn't seem to stop himself from gnawing down more trees and using them to patch and re-patch the dam. Every time he thought he heard water running, he patched the dam again, even though it didn't have any holes.

Norma could not understand why Phil acted this way. It got so that all Phil could think about was running water, and all he ever did was to patch and re-patch the dam, over and over and over again. Norma asked Dr. Dan, the Ashland Zoo veterinarian, what to do about Phil's strange behavior.

"Perhaps Dr. Deutsch, the zoo's psychologist, could help Phil," suggested Dr. Dan. "Let's talk to Phil about seeing Dr. Deutsch."

"I'm not sure I want to go," Phil answered. "Some of my friends here call Dr. Deutsch a 'shrink.' I don't know what that means, but it sounds pretty bad."

Dr. Dan smiled. "Dr. Deutsch is very good at listening," he said. "He really pays attention when you tell him about what's bothering you. He's great at talking with the animals about their problems, and helping them to make good changes in their lives."

Norma told Phil, "Dr. Deutsch has helped many beavers and other animals in the zoo when they had problems. Some animals just like to talk to him, even when nothing's bothering them."

"Well, I guess it wouldn't hurt to go see him," Phil said.

Dr. Deutsch turned out to be a very good listener. Phil told him all about his problem with patching.

"Your life will be better when you don't have to spend all your time patching dams and thinking about running water," Dr. Deutsch said.

"That's true," Phil agreed. "I'd really rather spend my time on fun stuff, like swimming."

"Would it be all right if we work together to help you solve the problem with the patching and re-patching?" asked Dr. Deutsch.

That made Phil smile. Beavers have very big teeth, so they have big, toothy smiles. Phil liked Dr. Deutsch, even if he was a shrink—whatever that was. Phil still didn't know.

Dr. Deutsch asked Phil to tell him about the problem he used to have.

Phil said, "When I think about running water, all I want to do is patch and re-patch that dam."

Dr. Deutsch said, "I want to hear about the times you thought about running water, but didn't patch the dam."

Phil quickly replied, "But that never happens. I always patch the dam when I think I hear water running."

"Hmmmmm," said Dr. Deutsch. "I am confused. You and Norma live in a pond you made by building a dam on the stream. You are always around running water, but you are not always, every minute, patching the dam. Right?"

Phil nodded.

"Tell me about the times when you hear water running, and you don't feel like you have to patch and re-patch—the times when it is happening even a little bit now," said Dr. Deutsch.

"Well," replied Phil, "when I am in the woods at the edge of the pond playing hide and seek, and I hear somebody coming, I hurry to my plunge hole. That's a secret tunnel that takes me all the way from the shore down into the safety of the pond and my lodge."

"You are a very clever beaver!" Dr. Deutsch exclaimed.

"I love playing hide and seek and swimming underwater, because I can hold my breath for a very long time," Phil told him.

"Oh," said Dr. Deutsch, **"so you can go without needing to** breathe for a **very long time**. I wonder

when you will discover **now** that your brain is the boss of your body. Your brain is where your imagination lives, and your brain can do amazing things. I wonder if today will be the day when you will take the times when you heard water, but didn't need to think about it, or feel that you had to patch the dam, and make those times bigger and longer, like a balloon getting bigger and bigger. That's right. Very good. Now, take the time when you kept thinking about water running, and patching and re-patching, and shrink it. The time of patching and re-patching is getting smaller and smaller, shrinking and shrinking. That's right. Excellent. Shrinking. Smaller and smaller."

Dr. Deutsch said, "I wonder if you would like to experience hypnosis now, or just relax and enjoy what you are experiencing. Perhaps you will enjoy imagining diving **deep down** into the water. Good. Go **deeper** still. This is a very **deep** pond, and you are very good at **controlling** your breath. You feel **calm, comfortable**, and **in control**, going **deeper**, noticing everything about this special, happy place, just enjoying the magic of your imagination and of this place. In the distance, you may hear the sound of running water. It will be interesting to notice how little it needs to bother or disturb you, because when you

are this relaxed and comfortable, there is no need to patch any dams. Just enjoy swimming, and the **deep, relaxing** pond."

Phil told Dr. Deutsch all about his "happy place" in the pond, and how much fun he had there.

Dr. Deutsch asked Phil, "Would it be okay if, in the future, anytime you hear or think about running water, that you could go right back to your happy place in your imagination? It will be fun to discover that just thinking about this **happy place** makes you feel so **relaxed, comfortable**, and **in control** that you won't need to patch anything, and that each time you practice this, it becomes **easier** and **easier**."

Dr. Deutsch asked Phil to imagine his favorite smell. Phil liked the smell of pine the best.

Dr. Deutsch suggested, "Whenever you need to feel more comfortable, or in control, all you need to do, no matter where or when, all you ever need to do, is to smell that favorite smell, to breathe in that pine smell, and those feelings of comfort and control will wash over you like the water as you dive down into the pond. You can continue to learn what you need to know to do to control what you never knew you could."

Phil liked practicing his new imagination skills. His favorite was shrinking the time of patching and re-patching that Dr. Deutsch had taught him. Now he knew why they called Dr. Deutsch a "Shrink!" He had helped Phil shrink his problems like an icicle in the sunshine. A shrink was a good thing, a very good thing.

# Olafur Ostrich

Olafur was an ostrich who lived at the Ashland Zoo. He was a very large and handsome bird. He could run very fast on his long and powerful legs, but he could not fly.

Olafur had a lot of tummy aches and problems with his poops. Sometimes his stomach hurt and his poops would be watery and squishy. At other times, his poops would be hard, almost like little stones, and his tummy would hurt then, too. When Olafur felt nervous or got worried about something, the problems got even worse.

Dr. Dan, the Ashland Zoo veterinarian, examined the ostrich very carefully and sent him for some special tests. After the tests, Dr. Dan told Olafur, "You do have a problem in your intestines. We call it irritable bowel syndrome."

"What's that?" asked Olafur.

"It means," said Dr. Dan, "that sometimes the insides of your intestines get irritated and sore and twitchy."

"They're sore alright," said Olafur. "Is there anything I can do to feel better?"

"The most important things you can do are to eat many different kinds of good, healthy foods, and take time every day to poop," said Dr. Dan. "Sometimes, you might need to take medicine."

"I can do that," Olafur said.

"There is something else you can do to give yourself even more comfort," said Dr. Dan. "You can learn to use hypnosis to help yourself."

"What's hypnosis?" Olafur asked.

"It's a way of using your imagination to feel better," Dr. Dan replied. "I'll show you how it works."

"Okay," said Olafur, "I'm ready."

Ostriches have very big eyes with very long eyelashes.

"Think about your eyelids," said Dr. Dan.

"I'm thinking," said Olafur.

"You might notice how **very heavy** your eyelids are becoming," said Dr. Dan.

Olafur's eyelids began to droop. They felt so heavy he couldn't keep them open.

As soon as the ostrich's eyes closed, Dr. Dan said, "Now your eyes feel as if glue were sticking them shut, **comfortably** closed, **heavy** and **relaxed**. When you are absolutely sure that your eyelids are glued shut, you may try to open them, but you may find that they are just too comfortably closed to bother."

As Olafur felt all of his body relaxing, Dr Dan said, "That's fine, just relax **more** and more **deeply**."

His voice was very soothing. "Imagine a warm summer day. You have an ice cream cone. It is your favorite flavor, but this is very special ice cream. It will coat your whole intestines with cool comfort. Feel it now melting . . . **soothing** . . . **coating** your whole intestines with **comfort**. Feel that comfort spreading down deep into your belly, coating and soothing your intestines. That's right, a strong, powerful ice cream coating is protecting your intestines from discomfort, letting only **pleasant** sensations come through.

"You will probably notice **now** and then, more and **more**, from day to day, as you relax deeper and **deeper**, how **comfortable** your tummy is, **feeling** only **pleasant** sensations."

Olafur's tummy felt quiet, like a summer day.

"It is such a beautiful day," said Dr. Dan. "Imagine going to a beach. See the beautiful blue sky. Feel the warmth of the sun, the cool **comfort** of an ocean breeze. Listen for the rhythm of the waves, **gently** lapping at the shore. It is a quiet, natural rhythm. Breathe in that natural, **quiet** rhythm. Breathe in that **comfort**.

"As you wander down the beach, a gentle breeze is encouraging you to go forward. You see a beautiful seashell lying in the sand. Notice the inside of the shell, how cool and smooth and pink it is. The outside of the shell is strong and solid; the inside is smooth and pink.

"Further down the beach is a little house. The walls are strong and thick. The little house is there to protect you in case of a storm. It's **safe** and **comfortable** inside. You will find a round knob. It is a dimmer switch. As you turn the knob, the dimmer switch blocks out any uncomfortable sensations. It is interesting to discover that, as you turn the dimmer switch **down** some more, the inside of the shelter turns a pleasant pink, giving you a comforting, **relaxed** feeling. You are far away from anything bothersome, far away from any discomfort. Let your whole body continue to soak up this feeling of **soothing**, natural **comfort**. You feel **more** and more **relaxed**, more perfectly **comfortable** inside. Your intestines stay **calm** and **comfortable** … healthy … pink … relaxed, functioning with a healthy, comfortable, natural rhythm.

"As you return from your pleasant daydream, bring those **good, calm** and **comfortable** feelings back with you, knowing that you can and will return to this place of comfort anytime you want or need to. It is a place that is always inside you. Those good feelings that you bring back with you will stay with you far longer than you ever imagined."

Olafur smiled, and as his huge eyes began to open, Dr. Dan said, "Now, remember to feel very proud that you were able to give yourself and your tummy an amazing amount of comfort."

"That was great fun," Olafur said. "Next time I go to the beach in my imagination, I'm going to pretend to fly with the seagulls."

Dr. Dan chuckled. "That would be something to see! And if you can fly, I'm glad to see that you have your poops in such good control."

# Spiegel Eagle

Spiegel was a bald eagle. Bald eagles are expert hunters, and one of the biggest and most powerful birds in the world. Spiegel and his sister lived in a very large nest on the side of a cliff overlooking the ocean. Spiegel's mom and dad had built the nest out of leaves and sticks. It was ten feet wide.

In Alaska, where Spiegel grew up, he was king of the sky. Alaska was big and wide and wonderful. Spiegel loved to soar above the mountains at the edge of the sea. His very favorite food was salmon. He would dive down into the water and catch the fish with his powerful claws.

Sometimes, Spiegel had trouble breathing. He coughed and wheezed. He had asthma. The frigid winter air of Alaska made the eagle's asthma worse, so he decided to fly south. He knew that the Ashland Zoo welcomes birds that are passing through. The zoo calls these visitors "hitch hikers," or "freeloaders." Harry, the Hypno-potamus, was the first animal Spiegel met at the zoo. Harry told Spiegel that he should meet Dr. Dan, the zoo's veterinarian, because he would know

how to help the eagle with his asthma.

Dr. Dan gave Spiegel a very careful check-up. Afterward, he put some medicine in a machine called a "nebulizer." The machine created a medicated mist that Spiegel breathed into his lungs.

"We call this "an updraft treatment,'" Dr. Dan said.

"Updrafts?" said Spiegel. "We have updrafts in Alaska, too. They're wind currents. I love updrafts. I can glide and soar on updrafts for hours."

"That's great," Dr. Dan replied. "Perhaps you would like to imagine that you are back in Alaska, soaring over the mountains, where you had no problem with that wheezing. When you get to that place in your mind, notice how good you feel, how **easy** it is to breathe in and out. As you imagine flying high in the sky, perhaps you will notice how **relaxed** all of your outside muscles are becoming. Allow that relaxation to go **deeper** still as your inside muscles **relax**, especially all those little muscles around your air tubes—relaxed and **comfortable**, soft and **loose**. This allows those air

tubes to open wide, so that all the air you need flows easily in and out."

Dr. Dan suggested, "Perhaps you would like to go on a journey, in your imagination, through the inside of your body and into your lungs, noticing how smooth and fresh and clean your lungs are."

Each air passage got bigger as Spiegel passed through. He could feel the air moving in and out very easily. As Spiegel began to fly down one of the tubes, his passage was blocked by a big glob of mucous. "Not to worry", he said to himself, as he imagined throwing into the tube a wing full of munchey-munchers. The munchers were like little Pacmen. They rode around on bubbles of medicine, gobbling up mucous and junk. In no time, the munchey-munchers had Spiegel's air tubes all cleared. It was interesting to notice how much more easily the medicine bubbles carrying the munchey-munchers moved through the tubes in Spiegel's lungs when he was nicely relaxed and comfortable.

Since it was Spiegel's imagination, and he could imagine anything he wanted, the eagle turned his imaginary calendar-clock ahead. He imagined it was the next summer. He had grown a little bigger, and he felt great. His asthma hadn't bothered him in a very long time. He needed a lot less medicine because he was able to relax the muscles in his lungs by using his imagination, expanding all those air tubes, making it easy for the air to go in and out.

Each time that Spiegel practiced what Dr. Dan had taught him, breathing became easier and easier. He brought that easy-breathing feeling back with him. The computer in Spiegel's brain made it really work and happen. The eagle learned that, in his imagination, he could program that computer to make all the right adjustments necessary to open those breathing tubes to help the asthma that used to bother him. That way, even less medicine could now work even more, even better, even faster. Soon, the only updraft Spiegel needed was the updraft of the wind as it lifted him even higher over the snow-covered mountains of Alaska.

# Mutter Moose and Elgan Elk

Mutter Moose couldn't wait to be as big as his dad and have beautiful, long antlers just like Daddy Moose's. Each year, Mutter's dad lost his antlers in the fall. In the spring, they grew back even bigger.

Mutter had diabetes. His best friend, an elk named Elgan, had epilepsy. When they were babies, the two friends came from Alaska to live at the Ashland Zoo.

A part of Mutter's body, called the pancreas, didn't work right. His pancreas didn't make enough insulin. Insulin helps your body to use food so it will give you energy.

Sometimes, a tiny part of Elgan's brain would get the electrical messages to his nervous system all mixed up. When that happened, Elgan would have a seizure. He would faint, and his body would shake and tremble.

Elgan took a special medicine so that he wouldn't have seizures. He had to remember to take it three times every day. Elgan hated taking medicine. It made him feel different from the other animals. He hated being an epileptic.

Mutter told Elgan, "You are lucky. You can take your medicine in a pill. Diabetics have to take their medicine in a needle. I have to give myself a shot two or three times every day. I have to prick myself with a different kind of needle to see how much sugar is in my blood, and I can eat only healthy foods."

"I'm tired of giving myself shots," said Mutter.

"I'm tired of taking pills," said Elgan.

"I want to eat desert, just like everybody else," Mutter said.

"Breakfast is boring, boring, boring," Elgan said. "I don't want to eat it anymore. I want to stay up late and have fun, like the other elks."

So they did that. The moose and the elk stopped taking care of their bodies and their health. Mutter stopped checking his blood sugar and giving himself his insulin shots. He drank a big soda, and he ate a candy bar. Elgan stopped taking his medicine, forgot to eat, and stayed up all night. Very quickly, Mutter got very sick and had to go to the hospital. Elgan began

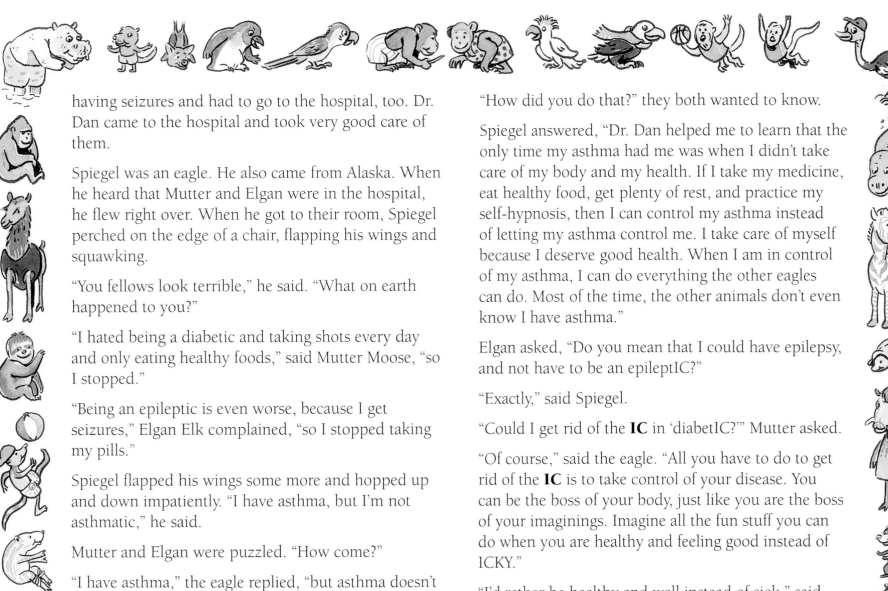

having seizures and had to go to the hospital, too. Dr. Dan came to the hospital and took very good care of them.

Spiegel was an eagle. He also came from Alaska. When he heard that Mutter and Elgan were in the hospital, he flew right over. When he got to their room, Spiegel perched on the edge of a chair, flapping his wings and squawking.

"You fellows look terrible," he said. "What on earth happened to you?"

"I hated being a diabetic and taking shots every day and only eating healthy foods," said Mutter Moose, "so I stopped."

"Being an epileptic is even worse, because I get seizures," Elgan Elk complained, "so I stopped taking my pills."

Spiegel flapped his wings some more and hopped up and down impatiently. "I have asthma, but I'm not asthmatic," he said.

Mutter and Elgan were puzzled. "How come?"

"I have asthma," the eagle replied, "but asthma doesn't have me. I got rid of the 'IC' in 'asthmatIC'. I don't want to be an IC."

"How did you do that?" they both wanted to know.

Spiegel answered, "Dr. Dan helped me to learn that the only time my asthma had me was when I didn't take care of my body and my health. If I take my medicine, eat healthy food, get plenty of rest, and practice my self-hypnosis, then I can control my asthma instead of letting my asthma control me. I take care of myself because I deserve good health. When I am in control of my asthma, I can do everything the other eagles can do. Most of the time, the other animals don't even know I have asthma."

Elgan asked, "Do you mean that I could have epilepsy, and not have to be an epileptIC?"

"Exactly," said Spiegel.

"Could I get rid of the IC in 'diabetIC?'" Mutter asked.

"Of course," said the eagle. "All you have to do to get rid of the IC is to take control of your disease. You can be the boss of your body, just like you are the boss of your imaginings. Imagine all the fun stuff you can do when you are healthy and feeling good instead of ICKY."

"I'd rather be healthy and well instead of sick," said Mutter.

"Me, too," Elgan agreed. "Hmmmm… s. **I. C.** k … That's where the **IC** came from. I'm definitely getting rid of the 'IC.'"

"Me, too," Mutter said.

The moose and the elk discovered that Spiegel was right: when they ate well, got lots of rest, and took their medicine, they were not sick; they were healthy. They could have fun just like the other animals at the Ashland Zoo.

And that is how they got the IC out of diabetic and epileptic.

# Lazarus Sloth

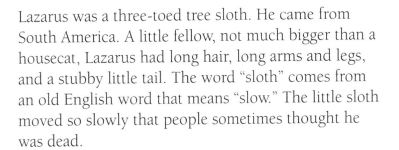

Lazarus was a three-toed tree sloth. He came from South America. A little fellow, not much bigger than a housecat, Lazarus had long hair, long arms and legs, and a stubby little tail. The word "sloth" comes from an old English word that means "slow." The little sloth moved so slowly that people sometimes thought he was dead.

Lazarus spent his days hanging upside down in a tree. It could take hours for him to move out to the end of a branch. That was fine with Lazarus—it gave him lots of time to think up jokes. He loved to make his friends laugh.

When Lazarus came to the Ashland Zoo, Dr. Dan, the zoo veterinarian, gave him a check-up. Afterward, Dr. Dan told Lazarus, "You have something wrong with your blood. The medical name for it is 'leukemia.'"

Lazarus blinked sleepily.

Dr. Dan explained, "The inside of your bones is like a factory. It manufactures white blood cells. For some reason, your factory decided to speed things up, and make tons of white blood cells really fast. It is trying to make so many so quickly, that it isn't doing a good job making any of them. Your white blood cells are coming out all wrong, and they don't work right."

Dr. Dan told Lazarus, "I need to do a bone marrow biopsy. I'm going to give you a wonderful, numbing medicine so you won't feel any pain. Afterward, I will put a needle into your hipbone, where the white blood cells are being made. I'll take out a tiny bit of the bone marrow through the needle, then I will study it to see what went wrong."

A very special nurse named Kathryn came to be with Lazarus while Dr. Dan did what needed to be done. She suggested, "Since you love to hang upside down, you could imagine that you are hanging in the tree tops and gently rocking back and forth."

As Lazarus rocked back and forth in his imagination, he noticed how calm, how comfortable, and how safe he felt.

Kathryn knew that Lazarus had a great sense of humor and loved to tell jokes and learn new ones, so she brought along a joke book.

"Why do hamburgers fly south for the winter?" the nurse asked the sloth.

Lazarus knew the answer: "Because they don't want to freeze their buns."

In his imagination, the little sloth saw hamburgers with wings flying south and toasting their buns on the beach.

Next, it was Lazarus's turn. "What do you call a skydiver who smokes?" he asked.

"I give up," answered Kathryn.

"A cough drop!" Lazarus responded triumphantly. Then he asked, "How do you know when it is time to go to the dentist? When Kathryn couldn't answer that one, either, the sloth said, "Tooth hurty!"

Lazarus was laughing so much that it tickled his funny bone right at the spot where Dr. Dan was doing the biopsy. His laughter even jiggled the branch where he was hanging upside down in his imagination.

After Dr. Dan took the biopsy, he told Lazarus, "I'm going to give you some medicine that will help you. It is a very strong medicine, called 'chemo', and it might make you feel tired and a little bit yucky before you get better."

The medicine went right into Lazarus's vein so it could travel everywhere in his body. Dr. Dan often had to take very small amounts of blood from Lazarus so he could see how well the medicine was working. That meant a needle. Lazarus didn't really like needles. Dr. Dan showed him how he could use his imagination to find the pain switch to shut off the pain from the needle poke.

Lazarus learned that his special "chemo" medicine was actually three different medicines mixed together. He imagined how each different medicine would work in his body to fight the leukemia. He imagined that one medicine was like a whole army of soldiers marching through his body and capturing all the enemy cells. One of the other medicines was like a Pacman traveling in his blood stream, munching all the bad cells.

Brownie, the bat, was one of Lazarus's best friends. Lazarus knew that Brownie could eat a huge number of pesky mosquitoes, but he never ate the good, beautiful butterflies. Brownie was an expert at finding

mosquitoes, even when they were trying to hide from him. Lazarus imagined Brownie flying through his body, killing only the pesky cells. He also visualized the factory inside his bones that made the white blood cells. He fired the old boss and hired a new one. The new boss made sure that the factory took its time, and only produced healthy, round, white blood cells in just the right amount. Lazarus noticed that when he was feeling all nice and relaxed, the medicine worked even better.

Sometimes, after the chemo, Lazarus didn't feel very good, and his tummy got upset. Dr. Dan asked him if he would like to speed up the time of discomfort. Sloths are the world's slowest mammals. Lazarus had never done anything fast in his life, so he thought speeding up sounded wonderful.

Dr. Dan reminded Lazarus, "In your imagination, anything is possible. In your imagination, you could find the super-sonic sloth speed-o-scope that can speed up your time of discomfort. You could also slow down your time of comfort, and make it last much longer by simply turning the super-sonic sloth speed-o-scope upside down."

Since slow and upside down was what Lazarus did best, this was the easiest part.

Usually, Lazarus's stomach liked being upside down, but sometimes, after chemo, it did flip-flops. Lazarus thought about his favorite food—the tender buds of a ceiba tree. He thought about being hungry, and how pleasant it was to eat the tender buds, filling his stomach with comfort, pushing out all the bad feelings.

Eating, like most everything else, reminded Lazarus of a joke. He said to Dr. Dan, "Three little pigs went into a restaurant. The waiter came over and asked them if they would like something to drink. The first little pig ordered a soda, the second little pig asked for chocolate milk, and the third little pig said, 'Water. Lots of water.'

"The waiter brought the little pigs their drinks, then he asked if they were ready to order their dinner. The first little pig ordered fish sticks, the second little pig had roast beef, and the third little pig said, 'I just want water, lots and lots of water.'

"After the little pigs finished their meals, the waiter came back to find out if they wanted dessert. The first little pig asked for ice cream, the second little pig ordered cookies, and the third pig said, 'Just water.'

"The waiter was very puzzled. He said to the third

little pig, 'We have wonderful food in this restaurant. Why did you only want water?'

"The third little pig said, 'Somebody has to go wee, wee, wee all the way home.'"

Lazarus remembered when he had told that joke to Harriet, the laughing hyena. Harriet laughed so hard that Lazarus giggled with glee just thinking about it.

Dr. Dan noticed that some of Lazarus's hair was beginning to fall out. Of course, that reminded Lazarus of another joke to tell Dr. Dan.

"Where do you take a sheep to get a haircut?" asked the sloth. When Dr. Dan shook his head, indicating that he didn't know, Lazarus told him, "A baabaa shop!"

Some days, Lazarus felt both happy and sad at the same time.

"That's okay," said Dr. Dan. Then he suggested, "You might enjoy turning the calendar ahead to when you are all better and completely healed. When you return to the present, bring those good feelings back with you—a present for yourself."

Then Dr. Dan said, "Don't forget, Lazarus you are going to do just fine. You have your wonderful sense of humor and your imagination—that's an unbeatable team."

# Lynch Coatimundi

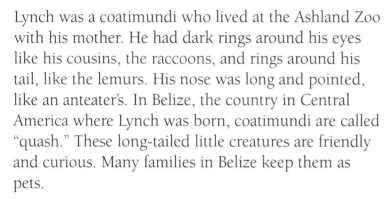

Lynch was a coatimundi who lived at the Ashland Zoo with his mother. He had dark rings around his eyes like his cousins, the raccoons, and rings around his tail, like the lemurs. His nose was long and pointed, like an anteater's. In Belize, the country in Central America where Lynch was born, coatimundi are called "quash." These long-tailed little creatures are friendly and curious. Many families in Belize keep them as pets.

After lunch, when the sun is high in the sky, quash like to take naps. Lynch, however, began to feel so tired that he also took naps after breakfast and dinner. Usually, the little quash loved to eat fruits, nuts, lizards, and bugs, but lately, he didn't feel like eating much of anything.

Lynch's mother got worried. She asked Dr. Dan, the zoo's veterinarian, to come and take a look at Lynch. After Dr. Dan examined Lynch very carefully, he ordered some special tests.

"The news is not good," Dr. Dan told Lynch's mother. "Lynch is very sick. Soon he will die."

Lynch felt scared and worried. He very much wanted to talk to somebody about his fears, but his family and friends found it hard to talk to Lynch about dying. It made them feel sad.

"I know two people you could talk to," Dr. Dan told Lynch. "Their names are Pat and Adrienne. Pat is a very special nurse, and Adrienne is a clinical social worker. I'll ask them to come and see you."

Pretty soon, the nurse and the social worker came to the den where Lynch and his family lived.

Pat told Lynch, "Your inside brain has a whole library of DVD and video recordings. On them your whole life is captured in memory. When you feel sad or lonely, it would be all right to pop in a videotape of a favorite memory, and watch it on the screen of your imagination. The tape might show a special birthday party, or maybe a wonderful vacation. It is your tape, and your imagination, so you can re-write a memory or change it. If there are parts you don't like, you can use your special remote to fast-forward through those parts."

147

"I remember a very happy birthday in Belize," said Lynch. "I was walking on the beach with my grandmama. The sky was blue, and the sun felt warm and wonderful. Little waves came running in from the big ocean to lick our feet."

The little coatimundi smiled. "Grandmama gave me a wonderful birthday gift. It was a fuzzy, yellow, stuffed doll. I loved that doll. I slept with it every night. One day the doll got lost. I miss my doll, and I miss my grandmama. She died. I like remembering that day on the beach. It makes me feel good inside."

Adrienne said, "Anytime you feel uncomfortable or worried, you can go back to that beach in your imagination. You can put any worries or discomfort into the sand at the beach, building up the sand pile as big as it needs to be to hold whatever you want to put there. If you have any fears, or aches, or pains you want to get rid of, put them in the sand, making the pile as big as it needs to be. When most—or all—of your worries and uncomfortable feelings are there in the sand, you will notice something interesting. The tide is beginning to turn, **to change**.

"The tide is coming in now. Each wave is getting closer and closer to the pile of sand that is holding the worries and discomfort that you, yourself, put there.

At first, the waves are nipping just a little around the bottom of the pile, and then a little more. Each wave is bringing in **comfort** and taking away fear. **In with relaxation**, out with tension and worries, each wave is taking a little more out to sea: **in with comfort**, out with stress and uncomfortable feelings. The pile is getting smaller and smaller, until it is completely gone, and the beach is smooth. Notice how good you feel, perhaps more free, like a very heavy burden that you have been carrying has been lifted, gone out to sea, and in its place is a **large** amount of **comfort**."

When Lynch remembered his fuzzy, yellow doll, he thought about other special things that he loved, and the friends and relatives he would like to give them to. It made him feel good to think that they would also have fun with these things and enjoy having them. Pat and Adrienne helped Lynch to write down everything he wanted to give away, and the names of the people who would receive these things.

As Lynch got weaker and weaker, he used his imagination more and more to do the things that his body no longer could. He went on wonderful trips in his imagination.

Death is the greatest trip; that is why it is saved for last. Lynch practiced imagining a beautiful hot-air

148

balloon, all the colors of the rainbow. As the balloon got closer and landed on the beach, he saw his grandmother and his lost yellow, fuzzy doll in the balloon's basket. They were waiting for him. Lynch climbed into the basket and they lifted off. All of the people in Lynch's family, his friends, and Pat and Adrienne waved good-bye as the hot-air balloon lifted up higher and higher, drifting farther and farther away. It was so peaceful, so wonderfully calm. When Lynch took his final breath he knew that the best trip had been saved for last.

# *Pam Penguin*

Sometimes, the visitors at the Ashland Zoo giggled when they saw Pam walk, because she had a funny waddle. Pam was an Emperor Penguin.

Pam lived with a lot of other penguins. Their home was called a "rookery."

Every day, visitors came there to watch the penguins. A big sign in front of the rookery said: "Please do not feed the penguins." Sometimes, the visitors didn't pay attention.

One day, a visitor threw a crab into the rookery. Pam thought the crab might be good to eat, so she swallowed it, shell and all. It tasted terrible. The crab's sharp claws made her tummy hurt. Pam squawked loudly.

Dr. Thom, the zoo's veterinary surgeon, came to examine Pam. He listened to Pam's heart with a stethoscope, and then he gently tapped her tummy gently. The surgeon frowned.

"You'll need an operation to get that crab out of your stomach," he said.

Pam had never had an operation before. She felt very scared.

Dr. Thom put away his stethoscope and sat down next to Pam.

"The doctors and nurses will take good care of you," he said. "They will give you some medicine that will make you go to sleep. While you are asleep, I will make a little opening in your tummy so I can take out the crab. After the crab is out I will sew up the little opening, and you will be as good as new."

"Will it hurt?" asked Pam.

"You will be in a very deep sleep," Dr. Thom answered. "You won't feel a thing."

"That's good," Pam said.

"After I finish the operation, you will wake up very slowly," Dr. Thom told her.

"Will my tummy be sore?" asked Pam.

"Your tummy might feel a little different while it is mending and healing," Dr. Thom explained, "but soon it will be all better."

Dr. Thom opened his doctor's bag. "I have a surprise for you," he said. He took out a small tape recorder. "Would you like to listen to a tape before and during the operation?"

"Oh, yes," said Pam. "That would be cool."

Dr. Thom smiled and began to speak into the tape recorder.

"You are a very special penguin," he said. Your legs are strong and your wings are strong. Best of all, you are strong inside. That inside strength will help make your surgery safe and easy."

"How can I do that?" asked Pam.

"You can imagine that you are in a special place," said Dr. Thom. "Where would you like to go in your imagination?"

"The sky!" cried Pam, and she clapped her wings together. "Penguins can't fly, so that is what I will do in my imagination."

"Let's practice," said Dr. Thom. "Close your eyes, take a deep breath, and away you go."

Up, up, up in the sky Pam soared. She flew high above the rookery. Looking down, she could see the entire

zoo. Higher and higher she flew, straight up into the clouds. At first, the clouds were white and fluffy, like the cotton candy visitors ate at the zoo, then Pam imagined the clouds were pink, her favorite color.

In her daydream, she could hear Dr. Thom speaking.

"While you are happy and relaxed in your special place," he said, "the nurses and I will prepare you for surgery. We will take good care of you. If you have any worried thoughts, put your worry on a cloud and let it float away.

"Pay attention only to the voice that is speaking directly to you. The voice will say your name. All the other sounds will seem far away, and they won't bother you. You may want to make the noises part of your daydream, or you could put the soft, cottony clouds in your ears, and only hear when someone is speaking right to you.

"If a voice asks you to do something, you will be able to do what it asks and still feel **happy** and **comfortable**. It will be interesting to notice, when you return to your daydream, that it will be even better than before, as you become **more** and **more** **relaxed**.

152

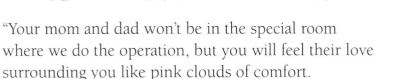

"Your mom and dad won't be in the special room where we do the operation, but you will feel their love surrounding you like pink clouds of comfort.

"You will feel the hug of a blood pressure cuff on your arm, and see a lot of special things that doctors and nurses use to keep you **safe** and **comfortable**, and help your operation go smoothly. You may notice that everyone in the operating room will be wearing a mask. That is so we don't get any germs in your tummy.

"Perhaps you will notice that each time that you take a very **deep** breath in and let the breath out, your muscles feel **more** and more **comfortable** and **relaxed**. Your body will feel very **calm**.

"Your blood is like a river. Whenever you are ready, you can bring the blood away from your tummy, where I will be operating, and send it to your toes and your wings. As the blood flows away from your tummy and into the other parts of your body you will feel more and **more comfortable**.

"When you are as **comfortable** and nicely **relaxed** as you are now, I will be able to fix your tummy. The doctors and nurses will take good care of you.

Your operation will soon be over and you will begin **healing** immediately.

"After the operation is over, you will start feeling better right away. You can continue to let the doctors and nurses take good care of you, but also know that you can do anything you need to in order to **increase** your **comfort**. Your body will automatically remember how to feel **comfortable** and to be hungry. You will wake up feeling rested, as you do after a good night's sleep. You will be so happy to be free of that crab and all the pain and worry that went with it.

"You will feel happy and pleased that everything went so well. The feelings in your tummy will be those of healing, and won't need to bother you. Your body is very good at knowing just how to mend. You can help your body to mend by remaining just as **comfortable** and **relaxed** as you are right now. When you wake up, take in a **deep** breath of **comfort**, filling your lungs and your body with **healing**.

"You will get better quickly, **completely**, and comfortably. You will look forward to eating and drinking. As you swallow, everything will go in one direction, straight **down**. The food will taste so good.

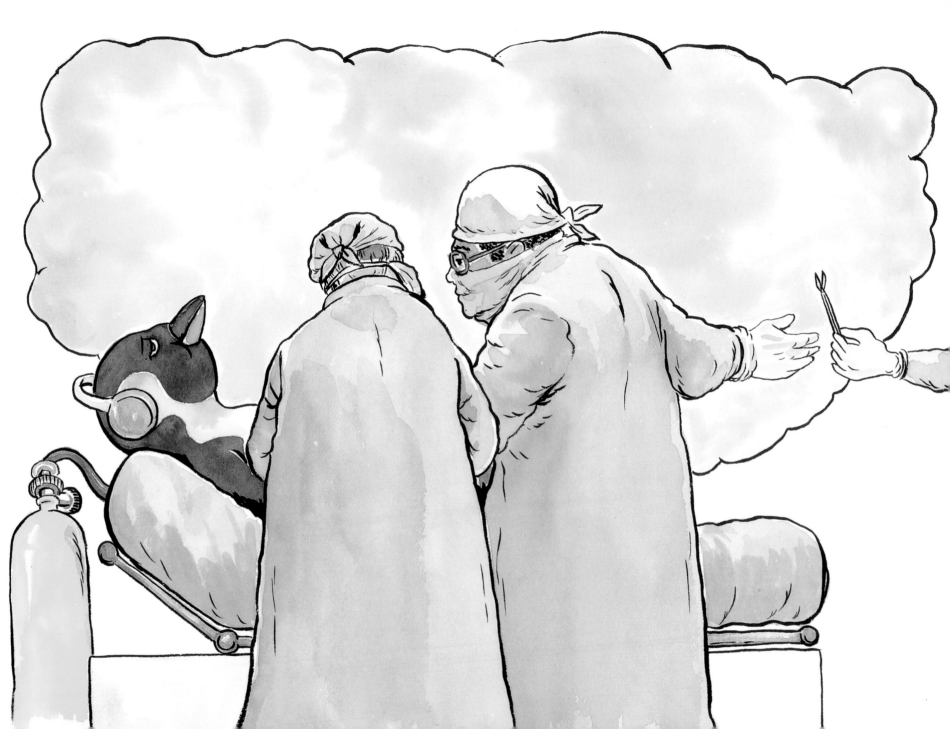

Your tummy will be happy to receive it. You will pee and poop easily after your operation.

"You can breathe deeply and easily. You will get better even faster than you thought you could. You will look forward to playing with all your friends. Your mom and dad will be happy to see how well you are healing, and how good you look. They will be proud of you. You can be very proud of yourself, too, because you can do anything you need to so you can make yourself **even more comfortable**.

"When you are this calm and relaxed, you will be **even more comfortable**, and you will **heal** very quickly. If the doctors or nurses need to give you any medicine, it will work even better when you are **calm** and **relaxed**.

"The only thing you need to do right now is to think about getting better, and **completely healed**. You may choose to remember to forget, or forget to remember, as much or as little of this experience as you want or need to, but you will remember to remember that you were able to give yourself an **amazing** amount of **comfort**, and then remember to feel very proud.

"Whenever you are ready to come back from this pleasant daydream, you will remember that you can go to your clouds of comfort and come back, bringing the happy comfort with you."

Pam listened to the tape, and her surgery went exactly as Dr. Thom said it would. Pam got better so fast, she was soon swimming with all her friends in the rookery. She knew that anytime she wanted or needed to, she could return to her pink clouds of comfort, and that made her feel happy and secure.

# Family Constellations

One day, all of the animals who lived at the Ashland Zoo began to talk about their families.

Allen Armadillo said, "I have three twin brothers. Actually, I'm one of a set of quadruplets—four identical brothers. We were all born on the same day, to the same mother, and we all look exactly alike. Armadillo mothers always have four identical babies: four boys, or four girls."

Allen continued, "I don't like having three brothers who look exactly like me. I want a new family. Brothers are okay, but I want some sisters, too. In my new family, there will be boys and girls. We will all look different from each other, and nobody will be the same age."

Amanda, who was a cuckoo bird, said, "I wish that I did look like my brothers and sisters."

Amanda's mother, Mrs. Cuckoo, didn't know how to take care of a baby, but she very much wanted her baby to grow up in a home full of love. To make sure that would happen, Mrs. Cuckoo laid her egg in another mother bird's nest. When Amanda hatched,

her new mother loved her adopted baby, and she cared for her just like her own baby birds, even though she didn't look like the rest of the family.

Olafur Ostrich said, "When my mom laid her eggs, it was my dad who looked after us eggs. After we hatched, he was the one who raised us."

"When I was an egg," said Pam Penguin, "my mother and my father took turns keeping me warm."

Norma and Phil Beaver told the others, "Both of our parents took care of us until we were old enough to leave the lodge and be on our own."

The eagle, Spiegel, said, "Both of my parents took care of me, too."

Candy Chimpanzee said, "That sounds nice. I knew who my dad was, but he never paid any special attention to me. My mother raised me pretty much all by herself."

Marshall was a marmoset monkey. "My father carried me around on his back all day," he said. "He only gave me back to my mother at feeding time."

"I never knew my dad," said Jordan Jaguar. "He left my mother before I was born."

"My mom likes to get married," said Ol'Ness Bunny, "so I have a new daddy every year."

Brenton was a tern. These small, dark birds live on the ocean. Terns only get married once, and they live together all of their lives.

"As a wedding present, my father brought my mother a gift of fish," said Brenton Tern. "That was my father's way of letting my mother know that he would always take good care of her."

George Hornbill, who was born in a tropical forest, said, "My mother found a hollow in a tree where she could lay her eggs. To keep them safe, my father cemented up the opening except for a tiny hole. After we hatched, my dad went to work looking for food. To feed us, he poked bugs and worms through that little opening in the tree. When I got bigger, and I was ready to leave the nest, my father pecked the hole open and taught me how to fly."

"My mom and dad loved me very much," said Sugar Man Meerkat. "They both had very important jobs, and they worked very hard. I didn't get to see my parents as much as I wanted. Babysitters raised me.

They took very good care of me, and I knew that they loved me, too."

"In my home," said Elkins Elephant, "all of the elephant mothers take turns watching each other's children."

Dr. Dan, the Ashland Zoo veterinarian, had been listening to the animal's stories. Finally, he said, "All of you came from very different families. There is one thing, though, that was the same for everybody: love. Each of you animals was special, and very much loved."

# It Makes a World of Difference

Lazarus, the three-toed sloth, was having a bad day. Dr. Dan, the Ashland Zoo veterinarian, was going to take pictures of all the animals. They had to be at the zoo lake at two PM. Early afternoon was a difficult time for Lazarus to keep an appointment, because sloths spend their days curled up in a ball, fast asleep. At night, they hang upside down from tree branches, moving very, very slowly from tree to tree. In order to get to the lake in time for the picture, Lazarus would have to get up at noon.

When the sloth got to the lake, everybody was already there. They had been waiting for Lazarus for the past half-hour, but nobody really minded. Their sleepy-looking friend with the long arms and a round tail like a doorknob was always late. However, when he did arrive, Lazarus always had a great story and a joke to tell.

There were no jokes that day. When Lazarus got to the lake, his wonderful sense of humor had entirely disappeared. He moped, hanging from a tree branch with his head tucked between his arms as if he were about to go to sleep.

Julie Giraffe, the only animal who was tall enough to reach him, loped over to the tree and whispered in Lazarus's ear, "Dear Lazarus, you look so sad. What's wrong, my friend?"

After a long while, Lazarus said, "I wish I weren't so slow. No matter how much I try to hurry—and I really did try today—I'm always late for everything. I want to be fast, like Milton."

Milton Cheetah was right beneath Lazarus's branch. When he heard what the sloth said, he sprang to the branch and crouched beside him.

"I'm surprised that you want to be like me," the cheetah said. "It's true that we cheetahs can run faster than any animal in the world, but you know, my friend, we have to. We cheetahs are very weak. Compared to our big cat cousins, like lions and tigers and jaguars, we cheetahs are the weakest of all. I want to be big and strong, like Harry the Hypno-potamus."

Harry, who had been having a wonderful swim in the lake, was passing right under the branch where Lazarus and Milton were sitting, so he heard what they said.

"I am strong," the hippo said, "but what good is strength when your eyesight isn't very good? I want to have sharp eyes like Spiegel Eagle."

When Harry said this, Spiegel was over on the lawn watching Jordan Jaguar entertain the children with his magic tricks. He could read Harry's lips with his eagle eye, so he flew over to join Lazarus and Milton on the tree branch.

"Eagles do have excellent vision," said Spiegel, "but have you ever heard one try to sing? It sounds awful! I wish I had a pretty voice like Wark. Then I could sing at the bird show."

By now, all of the animals had gathered around Lazarus, and everyone had something to say about what they didn't like about themselves.

"It's true that I can sing pretty well these days," said Wark. "But I'm so pale that, when I'm not singing, nobody notices me. I wish I were colorful, like Molly Macaw."

"A colorful coat is nice," said Molly, "but it doesn't help me fly at night, like Brownie Bat."

"I suppose it's a good thing that bats only go out when it's dark," said Brownie Bat. Nobody wants to snuggle up to a bat. I wish I were cute and cuddly, like Ol'Ness Bunny."

Although Ol'Ness didn't live at the zoo, and wouldn't be in the zoo picture, she had hopped over from her burrow to see what was going on.

"It's kind of you to say so," replied the rabbit politely, "but, you know, we bunnies are rather scatter-brained. I wish I were like Elkins Elephant. He's got a fantastic memory. That fellow never forgets a thing."

"I do remember a lot of things," said Elkins Elephant, "but I'd rather be quick and clever, like Max and Mitch Monkey."

"But we're not as smart as Candy and Cory Chimpanzee," said the monkeys.

"What good is being smart if you can't swim?" asked the chimps. "We want to be like Valerie Walrus."

"But Walruses can't cut down trees with their teeth, like Phil and Norma Beaver," said the walrus. "We have tusks, and we can use them to defend ourselves,

161

but they don't do anything really useful, like build a house."

"We can build good houses and dams," replied Phil and Norma, "but we would be able to do that a lot faster if we knew how to use tools like Oster Otter."

For the next several minutes, the animals discussed their shortcomings.

Sugar Man Meerkat wished he had a round fluffy tail like a rabbit. Ol'Ness thought things would be better if only she had big strong tusks like a warthog instead of whiskers. Marlene Warthog wanted to be graceful and affectionate, like a Thomson gazelle. Linda Gazelle wished she could be furry like a llama. Lonnie Llama longed to be as tall as a giraffe. Julie Giraffe wished that she could live in the treetops, like a sloth. Lazarus was astonished that anyone would wish to be like him.

Dr. Dan listened as all the animals wished they could be more like someone else. Finally, he said, "Remember Lynch Coatimundi? Some people thought he was an anteater because of his long nose. Others thought he was more like a lemur because he had a long, ringed tail. But he wasn't any of those things. Lynch was a quash, a coatimundi. He was himself. Each of you looks different and has different gifts and

things you are good at doing. You are special because you are you—just the way nature made you."

"You are absolutely right," said Harry the Hypno-potamus. "Everybody here is one-of-a-kind treasure. There isn't anybody like us in the whole, wide world."

When Dr. Dan took the picture, everyone was wearing a very big smile.

162